A Collection of Creative Writing

STORIES & POETRY

CREATIVE WORDS GROUP

OF EASTBOURNE

Copyright © 2023 Dee Rivers, Lorna Mason,
Vicki Adams, Keith Marsden, Myrtle Martin,
Anna Richards, Margaret Clare

All rights reserved.

ISBN:9798867665357

COMPILED BY

DEE RIVERS

CONTENTS

1	Spring & Summer	1
2	Autumn & Winter	12
3	Christmas & New Year	24
4	Acrostics & Poetry	32
5	Imagination	47
6	Nature	65
7	Descriptive Writing	72
8	Tongue Twisters	87
9	Dialogue	89
10	Our Short Stories	105

AUTHORS

Lorna Mason, Dee Rivers, Keith Marsden,
Anna Richards, Vicki Adams,
Margaret Clare, Myrtle Martin

MEMBERS OF THE CREATIVE WORDS GROUP
EASTBOURNE EAST SUSSEX

ABOUT THE CREATIVE WORDS GROUP

We are a group of like-minded friends who have joined together to enjoy producing the written word. We come from all walks of life, with varying degrees of experience but eager to learn the exciting art of story-telling. Some of us have attended writing courses that help us to share our knowledge with those who wish to take their writing skills further.

Possibly, the highlight of our time together was discovering our entries for a competition were included in an issue of the East Sussex Wildlife Trust magazine. The theme of the competition was 'Emergence' requiring 'something short and sweet, not more than 150 words.' We didn't win, but were delighted to see our words in print.

By compiling this book, Dee hopes to encourage those who doubt their writing ability, to continue putting their thoughts on the page and to let their imaginations soar.

The members of the Creative Words Group can proudly say, "I am a published author!"

CHAPTER ONE
SPRING & SUMMER

THE GREAT SYMPHONY TO JOY
Anna

The earth is awakening, nature stirs. The orchestra of Spring is tuning up, preparing to burst out into the great symphony of joy.

Bees buzz, frogs croak, animals groan at their birthing's. Birds' singing reaches a crescendo of pure joy.

Trees and flowers join in with their chorus of soft rainbow colours.

Everything is now in harmony.

So, listen, see, hear Spring's heavenly music. Enjoy every moment; all senses awakened.

SPRING IN WOBURN ABBEY
Vicki

We were going on a day coach trip to Woburn Abbey. It had been booked weeks before, so it was something we were all looking forward to, we being my friend, husband, and sister. We had been to Woburn Abbey before, but not at springtime, so it would look much different with all the flowers in bloom.

When we arrived, the first thing we did was to head for the loo's and managed to get there before others, missing the queue. We went in the Abbey and remembered some of the history, the statues, and paintings, after which we decided to explore the grounds.

Trees of all species, small, medium, and ever so tall, looking grand with their different-shaped leaves and even some tiny flower buds waiting to open up. The beds of vegetables were also ready to be picked. As we moved to the next garden, a greenhouse was noticeable and through the glass could be seen the most stunning sea of coral. We went to see what flower it was. It was the cactus in full bloom. Out-shining the rest of the plants.

WATCHING THE TIME
Lorna

"I'll watch the time", I said. We were sitting on a bench in the sunshine. It was springtime and the first daffodils were looking amazing. Bright splashes of colour along the centre flower bed in the paved, pedestrianised city centre. There was a slight breeze which disturbed the new green leaves in the trees, I thought, how promising and full of hope the scene was.

A gentleman had sat down at the other end of the bench. He had a walking stick and was wrapped up well, scarf and gloves, his collar turned up on his overcoat and wearing big boots.

"Is this the station?" He asked. Turning to me and blinking. A bit like a mole out of his hole.

"No", I said, a bit puzzled. "Are you waiting for a train?"

"Yes, I'm going home today".

"Very nice", I replied.

"Call a taxi, will you?" He stared about. "These people want to keep me in bed all day".

"You're OK to stay here for a while. I'll keep watch on the time. The train only comes at 11:30".

"Oh no, that's too late. 1130? Do you mean now or tonight? I can't wait that long".

"It's only tea time now, so we could go for a cuppa at the station".

So, we strolled along, arm in arm. Grandad and granddaughter.

THROUGH MY WINDOW
Dee

Grey clouds scudding this morning
Gulls swooping, screaming
Swallows darting across my view, whistling,
frantically chasing insects
An aerobatic show
Patches of blue, brighten the sky

Signs of summer
Now the sun breaks through
Enlivens the day
Rooks reel in the wind
Seems before long dusk descends
And peace prevails.

SPRING HAS SPRUNG
Keith

It is the season that both suddenly or slowly comes to life. We see it in the trees that for so long seemed dead and empty, suddenly produce blossoms and leaves. What seemed dead is very much alive.

In Christianity, we celebrate "new life". What seemed dead is alive again in the Easter story. In the Christian world, Lent and Easter cover this spring period, but for Jesus, these two periods were three years apart. Lent covers the 40 days when Jesus was in the wilderness of Judea after being recognised and baptised by John the Baptist to prepare for his ministry to his Jewish nation. Easter was at the end of his ministry, his execution by crucifixion and his resurrection from the tomb. Some Christians seek to follow Jesus by fasting and meditation during Lent (40 days) as a preparation for Easter.

I see a link with nature. What seems dead in nature during winter suddenly comes alive in spring. What seems dead in our lives can be changed to new life as we grow more and more in faith and love in Christ. However, we understand him! It is our Spring Joy.

WHEN SPRING IS HERE
Vicki

When Spring is here
everything comes alive.
You see in fields the deer.
Bees buzzing around the hive.
Daffodils and crocus appear.

Butterflies, Insects all around.
Can't help noticing trees
where the woodpecker's pound.
Making a nest. Seeing the leaves.

Miles full of splendour and zing,
knowing what life is about.
That's when we know it's spring
without a doubt.

THE JOY OF SPRING
Margaret

The joy of Spring.
New life. New growth.
New baby's tiny hands.
Tiny hands. All things new.
The adventure begins.
Resurrection!

FOUR SEASONS
Vicki

In Britain we have Four Seasons.
Summer and Autumn, Winter, and Spring.
Nature has no rhyme or reasons
for the wonder and beauty, it can bring.

Beautiful colours of flowers and trees
Enhance the scenery and views.
Insects fluttering and pollinating bees.
In the field sheep and ewes.

What a wonderful sight to behold!

SUMMER – FREEDOM & WARMTH
Keith

I feel that summer is the best season of the year. It is generally warm. Plants are becoming mature after their early growth of spring. The gardens and fields are at their best before the flowers turn to seed-pods and fruits. The animals, insects and birds, water-life are at their most active in their growing families and community groups.

All things and people are on the move to main holidays, relocations, learning new things like birds learning to fly, finding independence and interdependence. Then, preparing for the harder times, when autumn will inevitably come. Watch those bright green leaves turn brown and fall.

But for now - open wide your windows, as long as it isn't gale force winds. Go out in your summer clothes, as long as it's not raining. Walk the promenade, as long as it's not the time for Airborne!

SUMMER SOLSTICE
Lorna

Do you remember when
we stood together,
hand in hand,
in the grey morn light,
where the old stones stand?
It was all a great adventure then.
It was perfect weather with
so many there from
all across the land.
The first bright beam
over the Heel Stone,
then birdsong, then us –
A great gasp and sigh.
The collective energy
forever embedded in the mind.

THE GLORIOUS FLAMING SEASON
Anna

The glorious flaming season when Earth puts on her most vivid and sweet-smelling display. Spring was the opening scene, Summer the main body of the drama. Flowers and trees are putting on a splendid display; insects at their busiest, birds give their best vocal show and animals at their most active and reproductive period. Human's too with more energy and with time to be active and have fun.

The sun is making people more relaxed and happier. Children grow faster and enjoy the freedom of more time outside going on adventures, holidays, and the joy of being released from being educated and being constricted by educational rules. Teachers have a well-earned rest and recuperation too.

What fun to go paddling, have ice creams, experience holiday camps, going on fun fair rides, staying up late. Maybe visiting grandparents and being well spoilt while Mum and Dad have a wonderful break, if only for a few days. Special foods are on the table, like strawberries and cream, shellfish, and cold drinks. Less clothes and being able to play in the sand, have a boat ride. Each day having such fun and much too short.

We must enjoy every moment before the daylight begins to shorten and routine has to govern again and Autumn creeps in.

SUMMER MORNING
Lorna

Breathe in deeply.
Then slowly release.
We, the ocean, and I,
standing together
on the beach.
Pale yellow flocks of clouds

uplit against a Topaz sky
hold a seagull suspended
in sparkling light.
The sands seep and bubble
as wavelets retreat,
burying my feet.
One of a million uncountable
breaths, sighs. The Ocean and I.

SUMMER
Margaret

The warmth of the summer sun invites people to the shore to enjoy the sight of the clear blue millpond-like sea in all its vastness. The fishing, yachts and paddle boarding, a childhood memory in all of us. The warm breeze will dry them and their hair as they leave the sea.

Maybe they will walk the Downs to get an appetite up for dinner later at the hotel they are staying at. Or perhaps they prefer the park in full summer bloom, with squirrels waiting for some titbit. They count their blessings, as we all do.

The swimmers, walkers and sun-worshippers soak themselves in the glory of it all. We can respect and believe how small we are against our awesome seas, skies, hills, and nature generally.

Seaside towns are special places that swarm with visitors from all over the world. They simply love island life. It's not so far to go to find all you need to love life.

FREEDOM OF SUMMER
Vicki

At last, the warmer weather is upon us. With the feeling of the sun on my face, I know we have the freedom of summer. The smell of flowers with colours of many rainbows, trees full of leaves being different shapes and sizes, hedgerows keeping its prickles only adds to the beauty of the surroundings.

The green grass verges alive with insects, enjoying every nook and cranny.

Ponds come to life with frogs, waterlilies, dragonflies, and mayflies.

The blue sky brings swallows, swifts and even bats at dusk.

Bowling greens are at full swing, with men and women in white throwing bowls in competitions.

The beach is crowded with mums, dads and children building sandcastles and young lads eyeing up the girls in their bikinis who are trying to get a tan.

Families sitting in the pub gardens having lunch, couples in the park holding hands and friends playing cricket or ball games.

It's the time of the year when one can really get away for holidays to be ready for dark and cold in months to come.

SUMMER FREEDOM
Anna

The season of warmth, nature bursting out and life becoming easier. Freedom from having to dress up against cold weather, even if some days can be chilly. Birds are happier as food is so much more plentiful and less is needed to keep them warm. Plants bursting out from the darkness of the soil, sharing their joy by all their wonderful colours.

Sheep and cows are peaceful after their traumas of births. Even bugs are able to reproduce more freely. Even snails and slugs and flies. Butterflies breed and enjoy their lives, even if for only a short time. Bees buzzing with happiness, gathering nectar, are not having to rely on being fed with sugar, as in the winter months.

Children can run, chase, paddle, shout with few restrictions. Stretching. Growing. Enjoying being out of doors. Plenty of space for them to be noisy and roll around in the fresh air after being so restrained from having to be indoors. No school, few rules, and freedom to be themselves and develop their minds and bodies.

Grown-ups can relax in the sun. And take rest as stresses ease, a time of renewal in all aspects. Time to socialise, time to picnic. It's as though nature has opened her gates and wants us to enjoy her beauty bounties in all fullness. The time is short lived so revel in it whilst it is here. Hooray for summer.

MY TREEHOUSE
Keith

Well, it's now 12 noon, Thursday, May 12th. My flat is a little gloomy, but as I look through my three-paned window, the sun is shining very bright on the recently emerged young bright leaves of the Dutch Elm tree.

I feel I am in a rather modern treehouse - inside, modern furniture and fittings. Outside - I'm secured to substantial branches of my tree house. Through my window, I can see the depth of the tree branches and also other trees and beyond them the bright blue sky. I want to climb out of my window and climb through my trees.

CHAPTER TWO
AUTUMN & WINTER

AUTUMN
Vicki

Awesome
Uninhibited
Transformed
Unspoiled
Miracle
Nature

IT'S AUTUMN AGAIN
Keith

It's autumn again when the leaves on the tree outside my window turn golden yellow - take flight and leave their home and fly. They know not where!
Their going allows the fading rays of the sun's full range to light up my windows and my flat and my life!

AUTUMN PAVEMENTS
Dee

Brick, tarmac, slabs, all abound on the Autumn Pavements.

A breeze whispers lightly, the leaves dance around
in colours of gold, red, orange, and brown,
A gust of wind has them rushing down
to the Autumn Pavements.

A carpet of beach nuts crackle and snap on the Autumn Pavements.

Dead stalks of poppies litter the floor
where once swayed scarlet petals, they are no more
than a memory in my mind's store
as I walk the Autumn Pavements.

Strong weeds in the cracks still cling to their green on the Autumn Pavements.

I see a dropped tissue, watch it spin and swirl.
Hold my skirt down as it starts to whirl
as Sycamore helicopters twizzle and twirl
down to the Autumn Pavements.

Crimson berries in clusters so bright, lay down on the Autumn Pavements.

AUTUMN AIR IS FRESHENING
Anna

Air is freshening
Wind is gusting
Days dwindling
Nights darkening
Clothes thickening
Berries plumping
Birds fattening
Flowers fading
Children conkering
Cats are sleeping
Farmers reaping
Barns are filling
Harvest feasting
Folk dancing
Apples reddening
Forward-looking
Christmas coming

THOUGHTS OF AUTUMN
Keith

The change from long, light, warm days begins again.
The energy and light of the wonderful sun is cooling and darkening.
The time of harvesting and storing the food for winter is upon us.
Animals must be kept indoors before the bitter winter is upon us.

WE KNOW AUTUMN IS HERE
Vicki

We know Autumn is here
when leaves on pavements appear.
Leaving the branches bare
and the wind without a care.

Autumn means darker evenings to come.
Start of colder days and hum
of birds getting ready to migrate
to a much warmer climate.

Ground starts to go white.
Jack Frost seems to appear at night.
So, we know winter is on the way.
That's the end of making hay.

AUTUMN
Dee

Acorns cover the forest floor where the ancient Oaks grow
Unbelievable colours catch my eye as I scan the distant shore
Tumbling leaves drift across the landscape whirling and dancing
Under the grey sky, I wait for the rain to relieve the dryness of summer
Mist envelops the hills, hiding the view from sight
Nature prepares for the cold of the winter months to come

WINTER-FINGERS
Lorna

The champagne air,
       crisp and fair.
Long, low clouds ranging over fell and fen, gently
       Weeping. Mist and wind,
         gently sweeping.
Fresh wind, caressing leafless trees.
Soon icy winter-fingers
       bring out filigrees on each
       naked tree.
Frost and ice spangle
       branches against a
       pale blue sky
The winter sun shoots prisms-
Everywhere.

AUTUMN THE BEST TIME OF YEAR
Vicki

Some say Autumn is the best time of year.
Seeing the trees lose their leaves of many colours: gold, red, yellow, brown, and even faint green.
Everywhere is alive with the falling leaves and blooms of new life.
Once the leaves have fallen everything starts to look clear and lighter in the places
where trees hid the light to windows and paths.
It is great splendour to watch how Autumn changes the season.

FALLING LEAVES
Margaret

The falling leaves are drifting and floating in the light breeze.
It is so relaxing also such an opportunity for a gentle mindfulness moment
in an otherwise busy mundane day.
Take the time to see and feel the floatiness of each leaf 'til it finally lands,
quickly becoming a gardener's nightmare!
Blessed are those that live around trees in all the seasons.
Such wonderful reminders of the cycles of life.

THE DYING OF THE YEAR
Myrtle

Why do we fear death so? Or, if not fear, treat it as if it were not a part of life?
Death approaches as surely as the Autumn leaves begin to turn their colours and fall to the ground.
So, nature dies, the year drawing to a close, not in hidden sighs and behind secluded doorways. But, with howling winds and one final blaze of glory.
So, Autumn, with all her colours becomes the crowning of the year. Nature prepares herself for her little sleep and behind each fallen leaf hides the bud of next year's Spring.
Death is dead. It is but a little sleep, holding within itself the promise of resurrection.

AS AUTUMN APPROACHES
Anna

As Autumn approaches, nature puts on her final, fiery display. Leaves redden, turn golden. Flowers show off their finest colours: mauve, orange of Chrysanths, various colours through reds, mauves, and whites of the Fuchsias, the last of the Roses large and showy. All like a last carnival parade. The birds eagerly feast on any berries, fattening up for the cold to come. No young birds or young animals now. All preparing for harsher months.

I can feel my energy lessening as I too prepare for wearing thicker garments, staying in more. Almost looking forward to hibernation like the wild creatures.

There is much beauty around but it is not permanent. However, what is nicer than curling up with a book in my favourite chair, tea and toast or crumpet for tea. A short walk wrapped up on a sunny day. Christmas is coming, the days will begin to slowly light up and a whole new year waiting to be born.

One of my favourite times was being taken to Sheffield Park in autumn and taking photos of the flaming trees and bushes reflected in the lake with a gorgeous carpet of leaves around them on the grass. It made a nice birthday card. So, we must enjoy the. feast of colour and not feel sad of its passing. It happens every year. We must just enjoy the moment.

AUTUMN
Keith

All green leaves change to gold.
Under the ground, burrows are prepared for hibernation.
Time of light grows shorter.
Underclothes grow thicker.
Mother Nature is taking her rest.
Now is the dream time - planning the future.

The change from long, light, warm days begins again. The energy and light of the wonderful sun is cooling and darkening. The time of harvesting and storing the food for winter is upon us. Animals must be kept indoors before the bitter winter is upon us.

WINTER CHANGING
Lorna

Crashing waves. Angry seas.
Fury and anguish and violence.
Roaring wind, stinging rain,
hail, sleet, and deep snow
laying siege to the land.

Then silence.

Rage spent; chaos stilled.

Sparkling avenues of sun-embellished frosted trees –
a blessed sight.

Cinnamon, Vanilla, and cloves.
Star anise, orange zest, cranberries too -
mulled wine to warm the heart
with family and friends
and you.
Each season has many faces
just like you and me. It's true!

SHEFFIELD PARK IN AUTUMN
Anna

One of my favourite times was being taken to Sheffield Park in Autumn and taking photos of the flaming trees and bushes reflected in the lake, with a gorgeous carpet of leaves around them on the grass. It made a nice birthday card. So, we must enjoy this feast of colour and not feel sad at its passing. It happens every year. We must just enjoy the moment.

AUTUMN WARNING
Lorna

Golden oak and liquid amber leaves
Lie together on the fields.
The canopy overhead
Now shows soft skies, torn and worn,
Filigreed and laced -
No leaves.
But carpets now. Maroon and gold,
bronze and carmine,
yellow, purple, and brown

show the splendour of Autumn's
Fare in ripe berries and nuts
eaten with care.
Biting wind and slanting rain
bring thoughts of cold to come.
Hidden life will remain.

WITHDRAWAL AND HIBERNATION – WINTER
Vicki

With darker mornings and evenings approaching, we know winter is upon us and that is when the withdrawal starts. Plants are replaced by the hardy ones, which will bring colour to the coming months ahead. The trees are dormant so they can revitalise themselves, ready for warmer epoch to come. With the last hibernation of birds, mammals, and insects, all around us starts to go brown, making days seem shorter.

When the frost covers the ground, cars, and buildings, it looks like thin layers of snow. Then when it snows, everywhere is bright and we know it's time to get out the woollen scarves and fur boots and warm coats. At last, once again there will be tobogganing, ice skating, snowmen, and snowball fights. Black ice will be the danger, falling over, cars gliding everywhere, snow sliding from roofs, car engines not starting and steamed-up windows.

CHAPTER THREE
CHRISTMAS & NEW YEAR

A CHRISTMAS THOUGHT
Dee

Some people call Christmas 'Xmas'.
This makes me feel so sad.
It takes Christ out of this special time,
so, let's keep Christ in Christmas.
Make it the best you've had.

A LETTER TO SANTA
Myrtle

Dear Santa.

I'm writing to you with a strange request. I expect you get a lot of strange requests at this time of year. I have a list of things that I would like. World Peace for a start. And some new socks. My old ones have got holes in them.

The main thing, though, is that I would like to have proof that you actually exist. You see, I believed in you when I was a child, even though I'd never seen you. The stocking at the end of my bed was proof enough, and I trusted what I had been told about you. Then I grew up a bit, and the things I'd believed when I was small didn't seem so relevant. Older and wiser children told me you were a lie. Just a pretence to scare me into being a good girl. Just a story for little kids and simple minds to hang onto.

They told me that you were basically a legend, that maybe there was once a Saint Nicholas, a historical figure. But all the stories about you, that you are alive today and working to give gifts to all the children, well, that's all they are, stories. After all, there's no real evidence of you at the North Pole or anywhere that anyone has actually seen.

Then there's all those fake Santa's, look-alikes dressed up in shopping malls or riding the streets in Rotary Club sleighs. Is one of those the real you? And how would I recognise you? I saw one outside Tesco today but I was afraid to ask. And then I notice that he had a collecting tin. And then I thought, "Hang on a minute, isn't Santa supposed to be about giving? This one seems to be on the take!" There seems to be a culture about you and your elves these days that just wants to part me from my money!

Last year I watched the Santa Tracker on Google and I saw you chasing round the world, starting in Australia, and visiting all the countries of the world in a night. You were due over England around midnight GMT but I didn't see you. Even so, I was almost convinced. Then somebody told me it was all made-up. A computer-generated conspiracy to keep people believing in you and conforming to acceptable standards of behaviour.

So, my Christmas wish this year is that you prove to me that you actually exist. It would be nice if you turned up, although I'm not sure how you would convince me you're the real thing. Maybe you could answer some of my secret wishes, the ones I haven't told anybody else about. I'll leave the details to you, but you'd better be good.

Despite all my doubts, I'd rather like to know that the old beautiful story of the man who wants to shower the world with gifts to bring us all happiness is true. Because when I hear that story, something moves in me.

Yours hopefully,
Myrtle

A LETTER TO FATHER CHRISTMAS
Vicki

Dear Father Christmas,

My mummy and daddy take me to the pantomime at Christmas. My friend Rosie doesn't have a daddy. He is in heaven. Her mummy is very sad. Could you give my pantomime present to Rosie, my friend who lives at number 72? She has never been to a pantomime. And I would like a colouring book. Thank you, Santa,
Love Molly aged 6.

DEAR SANTA
Anna

Dear Santa.

Do you know where I am now? My name is Richard. I am 8. I lived in Ukraine in a small village. We were bombed out and lost everything. My Dad was killed but Mum managed to get us out to England. Some nice people in Manchester let us have two rooms in their house and look after us like a wonderful Noel present.

Please could I ask you to bring me some chocolate as I haven't had any for two years and can share it with Mum. I'd love some comics and a book about space travel.

Could I ask for a scarf and warm gloves please? Anything will do as we had to leave everything behind.

I will leave you a mince pie and some carrots for your reindeer.

A big hug and thank you.

Happy Noel, Richard.

A LETTER TO SANTA
Keith

Dear Santa.

Are you the Secret Santa we are all talking about just now? When presents just appear addressed to us individually but no sender's name.

In the first Christmas story - a baby appeared in Bethlehem with no father. Where's he from? Astrologers record he was a king. They believed it so much they travelled for miles to see him. But that put the wind up the present King Herod. He ordered the killing of babies.

The family of baby Jesus, Mary his mother and stepfather Joseph had to get out quick. They became refugees.

You never had that Santa, did you?

Where did you come from?

You magically appear every December, promising all sorts of presents and things, then vanish on Christmas morning, leaving fulfilled hopes or deep disappointment in your wake. Then to another long year. To build our hopes and plans for the future.

Keith

DEAR SANTA CLAUS
Dee

Dear Santa Claus.

Here we are again, that time of year. I'm writing this letter to you because we never get the chance to have a conversation as we move closer to the big day.

You've been working hard all year to make sure the children are happy. Thank goodness for our team of elves. And where would we be without the reindeer, especially Rudolph? He lights the way tirelessly.

Now, Santa Claus, please be very careful as you fly around the world. You are not as young as you used to be and all that Sherry and the mince pies, well, the evidence is there for all to see.

I'll have a big pot of hot soup and crusty bread

ready for your return.
Your loving wife,
Mrs Claus.

CHRISTMAS TIME
Vicki

Christmas time is so cheery and people dancing.
There are trees, baubles, lights, and glitter.
Everywhere, everybody is happy and prancing.
Even if the weather is be bitter.

Look forward to coming snow.
Building snowmen and sleighing.
As the winter gets colder, we know
you will hear the reindeer neighing.

THE WINTER FESTIVAL
Keith

Christmas is 'The Winter Festival'.
Imagine winter without Christmas.
Dead, dark and bleak.
Midwinter's day, December 21st.
The darkest, longest day.
But look! The sun is waking.
The days will now be lighter, louder.
Some may say the sun is reborn!
The Son of God?
"Rejoice! Sing, dance, be happy."
December 21st, that is more real for me than the controversial 25th. Why the 25th?

December 21st, the shortest day, first day of winter.
The light is coming.
"Rejoice! Sing. Dance. Give gifts to those in need!
Ho, Ho, Ho! It's Santa.
"Saint Nicholas bring light and life to our winter."

CHRISTMAS THOUGHTS
Lorna

Christmas has almost lost its meaning
when adverts and jingles began
In October, November, December.
Most of them being about mountains
of food, expensive jewellery, or new cars.
The carols ring out in joyous mood:
new versions, improved colouring for adverts,
post code lottery gets people hollering with glee.
Decorations, flashing lights and fireworks.
Even garden gnomes have a following.

But what of giving?
Having compassion?
Letting love flow?
This is the message
that brings a glow
when like minded
friends meet to
remember the holy
birth, long ago,
but not forgotten.

NEW BEGINNINGS & NEW RESOLUTIONS
Vicki

Twelve months brings new year, new beginnings.
Weddings, anniversaries, birthdays, holidays abroad for the first time, babies being born, visiting relations and friends who you haven't seen for a year.
Festivals, concerts, theatre, and cinema with new plots for stories.
Spring with all its colours and glory of new life and wildlife, making a show after hiding for so long.
Day trips to the beach where you haven't been before, to paddle in the sea.
Moving house or flat, buying property for the first time.
New hairstyles and colour.
Tattoos.
New car. You passed the test to be safe on the road.
Bigger CC motorbike.
Getting engaged
and last but not least, being ill and recovering.

New resolutions made and broken. Give up smoking, drinking too much, too many takeaways. Mow the lawn, dig out the weeds.
Spend more time together. Take the children to school more often. Take your son to football and daughter to dance lessons. Help more around the house, share the remote for TV. Take rubbish out instead of leaving it. Read Bedtime story every night.
Make breakfast as a treat. Attempt to cook lunch or

dinner, Not spend so much time tinkering in the garden shed. Sometimes take life seriously and not always a joke.

Resolutions are easy to say but so hard to keep.

CHAPTER FOUR
ACROSTICS & POETRY

KING CHARLES
Lorna

Kith and kin gather
In expectation of our
Nation's Coronation.
Grandeur for our new King.

Challenges awaiting
His birthright accepting
After years of training
Royal duties now awaiting
Lasting devotion, loving
Emotion streaming from
Soaring cheering

KING CHARLES
Keith

King of the Britons and Commonwealth.
I hope his reign with Camilla will be long.
New ideas of king and queen-ship will emerge.
Good leadership is what our nation needs.

Care for all in need must be paramount.
His concern for the natural world will develop.
Air which is clean will mean cleaning all things.
Royalty will change to more modern thinking.
Love for all will be developed.
Everyone will be recognised and accepted
Someday soon.

KING CHARLES
Margaret

Knowing his role
Inherited position since birth
Numerical order – the third
Greatness befalls him – of course

Contentment in his role
Harmony with the people and history
Alone, as has to be the case
Remarkable position in the country
Loving his Queen and his country
Elegant in his role as King
Sincere in his role and belief in the world.

KING CHARLES
Dee

Knights of old ride on speedy stallions
In Buckingham Palace Gardens, a tea party takes place
No privacy can be yours if you're a Princess
Ghostly corridors where ancient kings roam

Castles with turrets and flags aflying
Horses, black and white, pull the golden carriage down The Mall
Anne, a true Princess working hard for her people
Royal Queen's reign in state
Lords and Ladies attended the coronation
England **k**ings and queens have ruled the land for hundreds of years
Some people believe the monarchy should be dropped.

QUEEN
Keith

Queen for over seventy years
Unique smile which greeted every meeting
Elizabeth – the name my wife changed to from May
Everyone who met the queen fell under her charm, even ante-royalists
Never will we see her like again. She was unique!

KING CHARLES
Vicki

Keen on nature
Inspired by growth
Never forgetting the trees
Goes to church

Capable of helping the planet
Has desires to watch the seasons
Always keeping plants to produce
Rescues dying wildlife
Loves to talk to the flowers
Excellent with garden tools
Speciality, making things grow.

QUEEN ELIZABETH 11
Dee

Quintessentially British
Undoubtedly honest
Exquisitely elegant
Entirely loyal
Noble and wise

QUEEN
Margaret

Quality
Understanding
Energetic
Empathy
Natural

GARDEN
Keith

Green is dominant colour.
Arranged for effect.
Rain is its refreshment.
Drainage is essential.
Every plant is needed.
Now get digging!

BOOKS
Anna

Books relax me
Open new ideas
Out of this world
Keep me interested
Send me to sleep

CASTLE
Keith

Chainmail is my dress.
Arrows are my weapons
Shot from my trusted bow.
The Moat is my defence.
Long may my castle stand.
Enter by the drawbridge.

CASTLE
Anna

Crusaders
Against
Syrian
Tyrants
Leaving
England

CASTLE
Vicki

Castle with turrets
Aimlessly empty
Stones crumbling
Tilted to one side
Leaving the spaces alone
Empty of life

PENCIL
Dee

Pencil is ready
Eraser on its end
Need a sharpener now
Colour of the night
I use it every day
Let me be creative

CASTLE
Margaret

Cloisters are eerie
Alone in the dark
Some people like the feel
Totally unaware
Loneliness can kill
Every one of us.

SCUBA
Dee

Sea is deep and dark
Currents sweep around
Underwater diving
Breathing through tubes
Airways tight with pressure

HAMPER
Vicki

High tea for two
Apples and Oranges
Marg and bread
Pie with meat
Eat sumptuous
Rain, pack up

MUSIC
Dee

Moments in time
Utter harmony
Staccato pick pick
I sing with my piano
Chords ripple round the room

QUEEN ELIZABETH 11
Vicki

Queen Elizabeth the second reigned for seventy years.
Millions of us never, ever reckoned including earls,
dukes, and peers
that such devotion to our country would have an impact
on the people.
Nowhere was there a boundary, where Elizabeth made
us feel feeble.
Her smile and beautiful blue eyes always giving a warm
and content feeling.
In her stately homes and hallways. her voice so soft and
healing.

YOUR MAJESTY
Myrtle

Anointed Queen to serve your God and country,
Plainly dressed in white.
You made your vow to serve 'fore God Almighty,
In all humility,
Hidden from our sight.

We watched them take the crown and orb and sceptre,
Symbols of majesty.
Your coffin, bereft of queenly status, descending,
Ending as you began,
In simplicity.

Oh, may you rest in peace and rise in glory!
Our prayer for all God's saints.
The king you served in life, In-death will raise you,
Freed from human frailty,
Completion of faith.

Your God and King knew well the cost of service,
In his humanity.
In life, you sought to follow His example,
In death, He's your reward,
For your loyalty.

At home with Him and those who've gone before you,
United now in love.
Freed from the trappings of earthly royalty
And constraints of duty
In your true home above.

THE YOUNG LADY FROM HARROW
Margaret

There was a young lady from Harrow,
Who complained that her mouth was too narrow.
For times without number
She ate a cucumber
But she never could manage a marrow.

CURIOSITY KILLED THE CAT
Dee

My name is Baloo. I'm a British Shorthair cat.
I live with my humans in a Wimbledon flat.
To say that I'm loved, goes without saying
for all day long you'll find me laying
under a table or on the bed.
I'm a house-cat you see, it has to be said.

Not for me the wind and the rain, and no,
I certainly don't like the sound of snow.
My favourite thing is to lay flat on my back
Legs all akimbo; inhibitions I lack.
Scratch my ears, tickle my tum.
It's all I want and so much fun.

I don't ask questions; I don't tell lies.
I'm a Shorthair Blue with Amber eyes.
I'm lazy, I know, but I don't care
as long as my human is stroking my hair.
Curiosity killed the cat?
Not me. I'm much too cosy to be bothered with that.

MY THOUGHTS
Lorna

In everything we do, do it from the heart.
Be calm and observe. Do not have an opinion.
Allow others to follow their own paths.
If it is not in alignment with your heart, let it go.
Rise above all distractions.
Broaden our assumptions about others.

Allow your bravery to appear. Be authentic.

Grief allows the door to open for rebirth.
Change makes us feel disorientated.
Why are you alive?
Are you doing what you came to do,
or are you allowing someone to drive you?

Don't ever mistake my silence for ignorance.
My calmness for acceptance. And my kindness for weakness.

THE PRINCE AND THE QUEEN
Lorna

The man, so brave and strong
all day long to stand by
The queen, for her to lean on.
They – both beautiful
       both dutiful.
Who can compare?
We can only stand and stare
with eyes wet with tears
       of pride, joy, and loving care
for our Royal couple.

But now, the man so brave and strong
       lives on in our thoughts and prayers,
while she, brave Queen goes on
       alone, but not alone –
She wears a crown
       of love, compassion, protection.
The people's Sovereign Queen.

Still, she lingered on a little while,

        her final duties to deliver,
        until her body said,
"Rest now, dearly beloved one.
        You have walked the extra mile.
        You have fulfilled all duties.
Now with your blue eyes and lovely smile,
        it's time to let your young men rise
        to shoulder burdens you relinquish.
Your shining legacy leads them on
        as they in turn
reach for the skies."

As the Queen marked
        the pages of her life,
        her thoughts and feelings
        were captured for us,
        her people,
Long time hence, to touch and absorb.

CHAPTER FIVE
IMAGINATION

I THOUGHT I WAS ALONE
Keith

I thought I was alone, but I heard a strange sound. I stood looking down the staircase then advanced along the landing. A shadow crossed my path. It was a bat, flying across the moonlit window.

THE MURDER OF FAIRY PRINCESS ORLA
Dee

The sunbeams poured through the trees in shafts of dust-laden light. Spring in the Old Wood was bursting out of it's winter sleep. The leaves were so fresh, their iridescence so bright that one would stand in awe of the beauty of the place.

    Mr. Popplewood sat on his favourite leaf and surveyed his beloved neighbourhood. He wasn't foolish enough to think that this leaf would last a lifetime. No! He knew all about the changing seasons for he was the fount of wisdom for the whole area known as Old Wood, part of the domain of Northern Old Wood.

As he admired the view, smoking his pipe contentedly, Rudy Robin landed on the branch beside him.

'How do, Mr. Popplewood,' he chirped glumly.

Mr. Popplewood was jerked out of his contemplation. Looking round sharply, he asked, 'What's wrong Rudy? It's not like you to be glum.'

As he spoke a dark cloud slowly moved across the sun, filling the glade with a dismal aura. Mr. Popplewood shivered and Rudy Robin ruffled his feathers.

'There's something afoot,' whispered Rudy. 'I've heard on the grapevine that Princess Orla has been...' here Rudy lowered his voice even further and Mr Popplewood's large ears trembled, 'murdered. She was found in her bed in the early hours of this morning. In a pool of blood. Her beautiful throat slit from ear to ear. It's said that Queen Shaily is behind it. What are we going to do, Mr. Popplewood?'

'It seems that the dark cloud overhead is an omen of evil happenings. I must be off to call a meeting of the council.' With that, Mr Popplewood leapt off the leaf and with a twitch of his wings darted through the branches until Rudy could no longer see his glowing form.

Fairy King Elvy and his wife Queen Tanya were rulers of Northern Old Wood and its surrounding countryside. The king had been disturbed from his sleep by his number one dwarf, who later would have his left ear cut off for not waking him earlier. The castle was in uproar. The whole household (except for the king who had taken a potion before retiring for the night) had been woken by a blood-curdling scream coming from Princess Orla's bedroom. It hadn't been made by her but by the maid who had discovered her dead as a Dodo.

Every member of her retinue was called from their work to stand, quivering in the great hall. One by one they were questioned by the Kings' guards. No-one would admit to having seen or heard anything untoward during that night, consequently all were detained. They were forced to hover at arms-length away from one another until someone indicated that they had information. While the King sat on his golden throne, glaring at each of the underlings that hovered before him, the impish guards strolled along the ranks. After an agonising half hour, one of the fairies dropped down, her wings drooping dangerously near the floor. If her tears reached her wings, it would be a catastrophe. She wouldn't be able to fly for days, so how would she help her princess then. A new wave of tears began to fall when she remembered that her beloved princess wouldn't need a maid now.

'Pull yourself together, Violetta,' snapped a guard. 'What have you got to say for yourself?'

Violetta knew she must not look directly at her King, so she kept her head bowed as she spoke. 'I heard a rumour that Queen Shaily wanted Princess Orla dead. But I didn't believe it. I couldn't believe that anyone would want to kill our beautiful princess. And now, it's true. She's dead.' Another bout of wailing began, until the guard bellowed, 'Quiet before the King.'

The guard, puffed up with self-importance marched toward the King and bowed his head to the ground.

'I beg to speak, my King.'

The King nodded once.

The guard relayed what the maid had told him.

'Call Mr. Popplewood,' instructed the King to the guard.

'Call Mr. Popplewood,' yelled the guard to the dwarf.

'Call Mr. Popplewood,' boomed the dwarf to the raven who sat on the castle window ledge. The raven immediately stretched out his blue-black wings and soared high over the castle walls and out across the vast expanse of woodland towards Old Wood, twenty strayts south of Northern Old Wood.

Mr. Popplewood and his council of fifteen of the wisest fairies in Old Wood had been discussing this highly unusual problem for several hours. No-one had ever heard of anyone being murdered, not even Mr. Brack who was at least two hundred years old. The council were trying to outline the events but they knew so little that it was almost impossible. But 'impossible' was not a word in their dictionary so they were certain that they would get to the bottom of the puzzle of who killed their adored princess. Mr. Popplewood scanned his fellow councillors. 'Can I trust them?' He berated himself sternly. How could he question their loyalty? He had known them all of his 130 years. They had flown together throughout Old Wood and beyond on business countless times. But, never before had they had to deal with such a disaster as this. As these thoughts played back and forth, he was jolted back to the room with the sound of the raven arriving to give his summons from the King.

The council members realised that Mr.

Popplewood needed support for the mammoth task before him, so they rose as one to follow the raven back to the castle in Northern Old Wood. Their wings glistened like diamonds in the gloom of the cloud-laden sky. Like fireflies, they rose on the breeze to glide gracefully on their quest to solve the mystery. (to be continued)

I THOUGHT I WAS ALONE
Lorna

I had been writing in my room. Everything was quiet and I had thought I was alone. Small noises like the ticking of the old grandfather clock in the hall and the swish of rain against the window pane had a soporific effect on my eyelids. I had been rudely awoken by a noise.

"Was it part of my dream?" I shook my head, the dull sound reverberating round my brain, now wide awake.

I grabbed my torch and crept to the stairs. I stood at the top, looking down. The staircase was dimly lit by the street lights of the city. Nothing moved. Not a sound could I hear. I was about to step down when the old clock began to chime the hour, 1, 2, 3. My heart was beating a tattoo in my ears, my breath coming fast and ragged.

"Silly old clock," I thought. "You'll give me a heart attack one day."

Still nothing moved, still no sound. I tiptoed to the front door. It was locked and bolted. I went quietly along the passage, looking into each room as I passed. No window was open or broken. What could it have been? I found myself outside the kitchen, still gripping the torch. This was the last place an intruder could be hidden, and my nerves were stretched to breaking point.

I slowly pushed open the door. A shadow crossed my path, black against black, and a feeling of something brushing against my pyjama leg made me scream, drop the torch, and run to the stairs. I turned, looking back in fear to see what was following me.

"Meow?"

Of course, it was Satan, my black cat, who habitually bangs the cat door when he comes in.

OUR GARDEN
Vicki

Cath and Molly are sisters, Molly being three years older. Cath always had the outgoing nature and Molly, more quiet and shy. They lived in a semi-detached bungalow with three bedrooms, a conservatory which looked onto a small garden with a fish pond at the back. Neither sister married, both too busy with their lives. Molly was supervisor to 20 staff, making equipment for hospitals. Heart, blood pressure, and breathing machines. Molly loved her job and never had time for relationships. Cath was manager in a textile business, preparing all sorts of materials for dispatch to the clothing industries who made garments of clothing for the stores and shops. Cath did have a young man when she was in her early 30s, but misfortune stepped in and Gordon was killed in a car accident when a drunken driver swerved and hit his car, sending him head-on into a tree.

They both loved gardening and spent many hours in the garden pruning, planting, and watering.

Molly wanted to go to the garden centre to get some compost and a couple of pots for seedlings. Molly got a little peeved because the car wouldn't start so she called out to Cath, who was bending over the border tying some sticks to the climbing clematis.

"What's the matter, Molly? Why are you agitated?" shouted Cath.

"It's the car, it won't start and I wanted to go to Foyles to get the compost and pots. What are we going to do?"

Cath said "Don't get yourself in a tizzy. We'll call the AA and they'll come out to fix it."

"Say he can't get it going. What will we do with no car?"

"It'll be fine, you'll see."

Molly wanted the garden to be the best in the avenue to achieve the award of the year for best blooms and presentation.

"You sure they will be able to fix it? If we haven't got a car, we won't be able to go."

"It's OK the AA man is on his way," said Cath.

The mechanic arrived 30 minutes later and was done within 10 minutes. He said the sparking plugs were loose so they couldn't fire the starter.

"You'll be alright now." He was cheery and wished them good luck and went on his way.

"Now will you calm down, Molly? Let's go and get the pots and compost."

On the way home, it was late after having a bite to eat. They saw a young man, probably in his 20s, with a huge backpack. They decided to stop and ask where he was going and would he like a lift. The young man introduced himself as Matt and accepted the lift. On the way home, Matt chatted about his travels and that this was the last of his journey before starting college to get grades so he could be a football coach in America.

When they reached home, Cath said to Molly "While you put the car away, dear, I will take this nice young man to the kitchen and put the kettle on for a well-earned cup of tea and give Matt some of our homemade carrot and walnut cake."

Cath and Molly chatted away to Matt about how they have won the Horticultural Award for the best Garden the last two years. First year. Azaleas, second year Gladioli and this year, they're hoping, their Delphiniums.

A couple of days later, when they were watching the TV news, they heard that a hitchhiker had gone missing. "Third one in three years." Molly said to Cath. "I wonder if our garden blooms will win this year's Cup for the best Delphiniums. Last two years we had very good soil and compost, like this year!"

A MAGICAL FAIRYTALE
Lorna

Once upon a time in a land far, far away, there lived a noble King. He was brave and handsome and his people loved him. The Queen was the most beautiful woman in the land, not only in looks, for her golden hair floated around her head like a halo, but also in her good deeds. Their only daughter, Bella, took after her father in looks, long Auburn hair like burnished copper, was braided with flowers and her cornflower blue eyes were always laughing. She had her mother's energy and loved to dance, something that she was naturally very good at. Her friends called her Bellerina because she loved to pirouette wherever she went.

One fine day in spring, when the buds were bursting, the birds were singing and all the small animals in fields, woods and gardens were as happy as they could be, a handsome young Prince rode up the winding road to the castle. He had dark hair, almost black, but with flashes of blue lightning in it's folds when he tossed his head, looking from side to side at the beauty of the land and with excitement as he approached the castle. It too was looking splendid, with its soaring towers, hanging gardens - famous throughout the land, its many waterfalls shimmering like delicate lace as they played in the mountain crevices on which it was built.

The gates were flung open and trumpeters raised their long, shiny instruments, and a blast of tuneful greeting filled the air. The King and Queen stepped forward to greet the young man, while a groom stood ready to lead his magnificent steed away. With a flourish of his feathered hat, Prince Beauregard, who was rumoured to be the most good-looking and eligible man in the land, stepped forward and bowed with an elegant turn of ankle to greet his hosts.

There were cheers and singing, laughter and a great deal of merry chatter as the countryfolk surged forward to join the townsfolk as they all followed, at a respectful distance, the royal company. A magnificent banquet was spread out and everyone enjoyed the food and drink. Then the dancing and singing began as the afternoon turned to dusk and still the jubilation continued. At last children were taken home to bed and everyone from near or far slept a long and peaceful dreamless sleep.

When morning came, all sparkling with dew, and the sweet smell of spring flowers wafting on the breeze, an announcement was made from the castle. Belle and Beauregard were to be married, and there was great rejoicing. Standing on the balcony with the King and Queen, Belle looked deeply into Beau's dark brown eyes, the most beautiful eyes she had ever seen. They held hands, and after the speeches, waving at the crowds and looking shyly at each other, they leaned together for a sweetly endearing kiss to the cheers, whistles, and hurrahs of the people.

Now, as you know, in Fairy Tales there is always a cruel and wicked witch. Not five seconds after that kiss, which traditionally sealed the deal, a black column of stinking smoke landed with a tremendous crash of thunder and a blinding flash of light. Children began to cry and horror was written on everyone's face.

With a scream that hurt everyone's ears, their eyes streaming with the sulphurous ashes that were released on the crowd, the witch cackled, "I put a spell on you!"

Somewhere in the crowd, a single voice was heard to croak, "There must be a song in that?"

But now was not the time for singing as the wicked witch continued, "Everything in the land will die."

She lowered her voice to such a degree on the last word that it made her cough. People looked up at her, noticing the pustules on her nose, the dribble on her hairy chin, and the uneven, broken black teeth. She noticed the expressions of revulsion on their faces and knew what they were thinking. She brought her magic wand up over her head and another deafening crash of thunder, followed by an earth-shaking lightning strike shot down the road. Her hair turned white and stuck out, giving off waves of crackling electricity. Her eyebrows seemed to writhe like snakes, and there was a nauseating smell of burnt hair and flesh.

It was more than most could bear, and many simply fainted where they stood.

But a lone voice could be heard crying out, "There must be something that can change this."

"Oh, yes!" Screamed the witch with a mirthless cackle.

"There is." She pointed her wand, now completely carbonised at Belle and Beau.

"Belle will lie as dead." She paused as Belle slowly crumpled onto a couch, which happened to appear as if by magic.

"Until," she continued, "You," pointing the burnt branch at Beau, "Until you bring me what all women want."

A laugh which sounded like a turkey's gobble rolled out of her wide-open mouth.

"You have 100 years to find the answer. Only then will the spell be broken."

With that, she spun round in ever decreasing circles, burrowing into the scorched earth, and was gone. Anyone remaining alive slowly sank to the hard, black, and burnt ground and lay as dead.

Silence fell over the land. Beau turned, stepped, and stopped as a little cloud of ash rose around his feet. Where should he go? Who would help him? And who would know the answer to such a question?

It was now almost 100 years later, and although Beau had not aged, by some strange magic which he did not understand, he had still not found an answer to the question. Some said a ring upon her finger, some said a baby in her arms, some said wise and some said frivolous things. But none of the answers struck a bell, nor a warm feeling in his heart, which would be the indication that he felt would be the answer, the one true answer. A feeling of longing filled his thoughts. He remembered her bright hair, like burnished copper. Her cornflower blue eyes. The way she smiled and the gentle touch of her hand in his and he longed for her body, mind, and spirit. He had to go back, even if he didn't know the true answer. All he could do was to offer himself just as he was, because that was all he had. He had never stopped loving her and never would.

Today was the day that the 100 years was up and Beau led his horse slowly up the hill to the enchanted castle. Everywhere, everything was just as he last saw it, black and burned to ashes, except he could see a bright, burnished copper light. "Belle," he breathed, overcome with longing. "I've missed you so much."

Now he was filled with energy and gathered her sleeping form in his arms.

"I don't know the answer to the witch's question, but I do know that I have searched the earth for long, long years." He was almost sobbing. "I have nothing to give you," he swallowed painfully, dreading the punishment that would surely be wrought when the which appeared.

"My darling, I have nothing to give you, except myself, just as I am without an answer, but with all my love," he whispered brokenly as he kissed her cherry red lips.

There was a blinding flash of light and the sound of sighing and sleepy stirring as everywhere across the land, everything drew long, refreshing breaths, and life began again where it left off.

"Rise, Sir Beau!" Astonished, Beau and Belle sat

up and looked around. Before them stood an amazing apparition dressed in scintillating colours of the rainbow.

"I am your fairy godmother." She touched Belle with her wand, and Belle stood up beside Beau, both of them bathed in celestial light.

"You have laboured long," she said, touching Beau with her wand.

"You have remained faithful and true, and you have discovered many things along the way. You have a loyal and steadfast heart and it belongs to the woman you love and that is what all women want." As if by magic, the witches voice was heard throughout the land, and great cheers were heard near and far.

At last, the witch who was no longer a witch raised her wand for silence.

"My name is Grace." Little bells tinkled in tune with her voice. "The gift I give you is kindness and goodwill. Let go of things that do not matter and be grateful for all that does matter. Forgive one another and apologise for any hurt that you may cause. Be mindful and speak kindly. And above all, have compassion." With these words of wisdom, she was gone.

The very next day, Belle and Beau were married and lived happily ever after. They ruled the Kingdom wisely and well, and became famous in Fairyland and beyond for the happiness which flowed like milk and honey in abundance, and still does to this day.

THE MURDER THAT NEVER WAS!
Margaret

Her case was by the door. Julie was ready to respond to the e-mail from her friend Barbara. Something very strange was upsetting the people of Netherton Village. Barbara was reaching out to her for help. By the time she taxied to the nearest station, she was feeling more and more curious. After all, her friend was not a person to panic. She was a member of the WI, for goodness sake. In no time at all, she was on the train, with her imagination working overtime.

They would meet in the local pub, the Kings Head. She hadn't been there for years. She also booked a room there for a couple of days. Nothing had changed. Places like Netherton never changed! After a couple of gin and tonics, Barbara slowly poured out her story. Julie was stunned. What could be the cause of so many birds dying in the village? Dead birds were everywhere. A stranger story she'd yet to hear.

They decided to go to see Matilda. She was a well-known horticulturist. Well revered and trusted. People all over the world consulted her over their various issues. They pulled up outside the old cottage. It looked so isolated. They knocked at the door and received no response. Yet everyone said she would be home at this time. So, Julie said, "Let's go and see if she's in the back garden." Sadly, they saw even more birds. Worse still, as they pushed open the kitchen door, which was ajar, they both gasped in horror as they saw Matilda collapsed on the kitchen table. Barbara rushed to her and found she was stone dead with a look of agony on her face. She quickly phoned the local police to establish why she was killed. A mugging? The police arrived in 5 minutes. As it was an untimely death, it would be a big investigation. An autopsy followed, and it took a week to discover the cause of death.

In the meantime, Julie had moved in with Barbara until the situation was resolved. Everyone in the village was shocked and afraid. Unbelievably, the cause of death was Arsenic poisoning.

"What?" Cried Julie. "She didn't have any enemies. This can't be true."

At this point, the policeman stepped in. His name was Bob Sharpe. He said, "Before we go any further, we must do a full search of the outbuilding and areas, including every inch of the cottage. In case the source of contamination was actually here."

They all offered to help the police and so the search began. It was a thorough search which took two or three days.

Then suddenly, Julie cried out, "No one has looked under the sink yet." When they looked at it, all became very clear. The bottle of Arsenic was there and the top was leaking a bit from where she'd carefully used it, as she had for many years for the rats in the out-houses. To their amazement, enough had dripped after each use to dampen the bird seed that was next to it.

"So that was what was killing the birds," Barbara muttered almost to herself. In turn, when she had brought the bird seed to the kitchen surface to measure it out, her breadboard had become contaminated and she had poisoned herself. She must have been getting a bit lax. She'd had a wonderful career of care for nature and, at the age of 76, had made a fatal mistake.

"What a tragic end to a wonderful person's

life," Bob commented. "She'd always been so particular and cared so deeply for the birds and animals and all of nature. Just one lapse of judgement can only be put down to the fact she was entering an elder era. God bless you, Matilda, for all the good you did for Netherton all those years."

Julie smiled, "The village will miss her." In no time at all, she was on the train and headed home. She pondered on the fact that maybe she needed to do some safety checks of her own.

THE HOUSE
Keith.

The woman in the pale blue headscarf came out to meet the people who had gathered and were waiting on the main lawn outside the imposing front door. They had all come from various towns within easy reach of this grand house. The lady who greeted them had been the housekeeper at the house when it closed 150 years ago.

The last of the family who owned the house had died in a sea disaster. Their will had stated that the house had to stay as it was for 150 years, when the housekeeper would return and open the house to visitors. Until then, the house was to be locked up and only the garden was to be cared for. These wishes were kept and paid for from the legacy.

The people gathered on the lawn, were from various areas and had heard the story by many means, and had come to see what would happen after 150 years of closure.

On the anniversary date, that woman in the pale blue headscarf opened the main front door from the inside. She motioned to the people on the lawn to come to her. She led them into the house. Not everyone followed. Some went round the back. All other doors and windows were sealed and covered. When they returned to the front door, it too was locked and covered. When the police eventually got into the building, there was no one there. No footmarks in the dust and dirt of 150 years. Just how it had been left 150 years ago. All who had followed the lady with the pale blue headscarf were registered as missing persons. The question now is what to do with this house.

It is now a dark, neglected house. For now, no relatives or anyone are willing to take responsibility for it. The local authority wants to take it over and the estate around it.

The families of the missing persons and the remaining descendants of the original owners want it to be designated an official grave and 'Memorial to the Missing.'

A good outcome has been agreed to take down the house and all outbuildings and create a crematorium, a public Chapel, a graveyard, and a garden of remembrance for the whole community. This was completed five years ago! But all these facilities remain unused, except for the Garden of Remembrance, where the memorial to the Missing Persons always has a bunch of fresh flowers on its stone plinth.

It was sometime later that the Memorial

Garden to the Missing again made the national news. It had been a dark and stormy night. The report said that one of the old, tall trees, which had stood for years in the garden of the house and now surrounded the memorial garden, crashed to the ground, and split the flower-holding plinth. The stone plinth bled! Where the blood had come from, no one knew. But it ran down the sides of the plinth from the site of the split. It has been cleaned and restored now, but no flowers have been left there since the storm. Many local people now want the area to be "Wilded." Return it to its natural state. Forget "The House." Forget the "Missing."

LADY JANE'S GHOST
Myrtle

Things were always happening at Old Farm Manor. I've been sent to investigate and write a report for the local Gazette. Its circulation is falling and our esteemed editor is hoping that something sensational will improve sales. If things don't start looking up, he says, "you might as well fly me to the moon and let me float among the stars!" So, after this little excursion into the world of investigative journalism, we then plan to go for a drink and a meal at the Stag Inn to mull it over. A few beers and he'll be floating among the stars, I thought, but let's get this story written first. And so, as the shadows lengthen, I direct my feet to the sunny side of the street and set off for the long-deserted Manor. I pass the old school building that still stands just inside the Manor gates. It is said that at night a strange noise would float across the playground. Maybe I will return later to check it out.

Old Farm Manor House stands, perhaps unsurprisingly, at the edge of The Old Farm. Nobody quite knows how old the farm is. Some say it dates back to the Sixteenth Century, others put the date later, but all agree that it's haunted. The first recorded tenant of the farm was a chap called Paul. Paul played the trumpet, most unusual in his time. He had six children, a herd of Friesians and a homely wife. This homely wife, Jane, caught the eye of the Lord of the Manor, up at the big house. Farmer Paul was furious! Screaming obscenities, he dived at his Lordship, cutting his ear badly. It was a banana skin that caused him to fall and his Lordship bumped him off and made Jane his Lady. They say she haunts the Manor, searching for her first true love.

Well, so much for the history. I'm halfway across the first field now, on my way to the big house. It's boggy and hard going. The field has been used for keeping pigs for as long as anyone can remember. They're all gone now, of course, Even the prize pair, Pinky and Perky, that won all the local shows. And yet a smell lingers on the air. The wind is rising and I swear I can hear a squeaky voice. "Who is it?" I turned to see.

"Pinky! It's Pinky! I've lost my Perky!"

I see nothing, and in my haste to get away, I stumble and fall face down in a boggy, muddy patch of trampled grass. A thin laugh drifts on the wind.

"Wallowing in thick, gooey mud is just the best thing," says Pinky.

Now if I were a sensible man, I would end my story here with the words, "I turned and ran for my life." But nobody is going to accuse me of being faint-hearted. I'm already writing the story in my head. I've got the first line, "The wind howled, the trees threatened," and that's exactly how it's starting to feel right now! My heart is pounding after the whole pig-voice thing. Maybe I imagined it? I remember talking to my editor in the office as he searched for a YouTube video about haunted houses. Same kind of spooky voices wafting on the wind. It'll all be in my mind. Makes for a good yarn, though!

I'm at the house now, just looking through the windows, trying to see if I can get in. They say some school boys broke in a few years back. They were playing marbles across the hall floor when Lady Jane's ghost drifted down the staircase. Young Pete Smith dropped his satchel as all his marbles came crashing to the floor, leaving dirty marks on the carpet. They weren't the only marbles he lost that day; he has never been the same since. And the ghost of Lady Jane, her job done, slid into the shadows. She just left them standing there, walked away without a sound.

Thinking about it is actually freaking me out now! A couple of bats have flitted out through one of the upstairs windows and are silently flapping about my head. They're only Pipistrelles but when I write my story up, they will virtually become vampires! I start to back away. I think I can see a ghostly shape through the drawing room windows. I'm sure it's Lady Jane. Anyway, it will be, on the pages of The Gazette. The readers are going to love it, but I am going to leg it! I shall write a fine story and they will never know what happened!

CURIOSITY SAVED THE CAT
Anna

Tom was a farmer who shared the farm with his brother. Tom was fat, his brother lean. They kept pigs, which often broke free from their enclosure. Pinkie was the most frequent escapee.

Tom and his brother, John went searching for him one night. They heard a scampering in the bushes but no Pinkie. They searched around and even looked in the old derelict school grounds. It was a dark night. Very creepy. The school was reputed to be haunted. The gate creaked when they went through, making them feel quite scared. They saw a flickering blue light, so decided to disappear pronto. Hurrying back, John fell and hit his head on the kerb.

"Silly old me," he said.

A bit dizzy, he muttered for no reason, "I must build a boat and can sail away to a desert island."

Something he had always desired, but the blow must have stirred up his dream. Then they saw Pinkie in Mrs Ford's vegetable garden filling his belly!

They grabbed him and said, "you will be the next one to go. Always escaping."

But Pinkie had other ideas. The next time he escaped, a day later, he trotted over the hill and far away to the hippie commune. They were only vegetarians and made him very welcome. They looked after a collection of stray animals. A goat, cats, dogs, and a tortoise. So, the last laugh was on Pinkie. He was not going to be made into bacon! No way!

CHAPTER SIX
NATURE

EMERGENCE
Dee

I'd been sitting in my favourite spot in the woods listening to the spectacular dawn chorus. It was hard to believe what had happened as I looked around me. The surrounding ground had turned from green to blue and white as if by magic. When I'd arrived earlier the heads of the bluebells and wood anemones were drooping in the cool of the night and had gone unnoticed. All I could now see was a carpet of blue with the white stars of the wood anemones peeping in between. The flowers appeared to be dancing through the shadows and sunbeams.

    A wonderful morning. I felt alive with the miracle of it all. The birds had quietened now and I could make out the beginnings of the day as vehicles on the nearby road gathered momentum. People journeying to work and school. Ah well, back to life for another day.

EMERGENCE
Margaret

Such joy. They're here. The Snowdrops and the Daffodils. Emerging from Winter into Spring. The struggle to get through, to turn their faces to the sun. To live and breathe again in this wonderful season, to see colours of love and life, to feel such freedom of the soul. As the journey from the earth means to be able to see the sun and feel it on their faces!

Yes! We are one, nature and I. to gaze on the Snowdrops and Daffodils also other life springing into being. Joyous sights to behold as they settle into the breeze, being strong and brave.

EMERGENCE
Anna

I love the feel of the sun's warmth, warming the earth, animals, birds, and humans. One can experience new life emerging from earth's dark depths. Energy stirring. In the garden the plants are awakening, daffodils beginning to open, birds on trees stirring. Birds beginning to tune up for their first orchestral performance. Squirrels stirring, rooks squabbling and pilfering other rooks nesting materials. In the fields sheep and cows anxiously anticipating the ordeal of new birth. Showers are refreshing plants, grass, and filling ditches. Movement is everywhere. People passing each other are opening up and greeting even strangers, wanting to communicate and pass on their joy. Life is returning and we can bravely face the New Year with hope and expectation like no other time of year. All is renewed and freshly gifted to us all.

EMERGENCE
Lorna

The morning star,
Still bright in the sky,
Now hides in the mist
And from afar –
Yet, right by my side,
A question hangs in the air,
Delicate as a spider's web
Spangled with dew as
The sun's prisms
Shake off night's dreams –
And the chorus sings
From tiny throats –
Far and wide
Joy! Joy! To all!

EMERGENCE
Keith

I live in a third-floor apartment. The view from my window includes a lovely old Victorian school (built in 1840) which has been converted into a private house. Between my flat and the school house is a large Dutch Elm tree. I can see the house through the bare branches of the tree. As Spring and Summer approach, I know that leaves will have their "emergence." Lovely as they emerge and grow – but my view of that house (and other things) will gradually disappear behind a blanket of green and my flat will become darker in the day time. I look forward to leaf-fall in the Autumn, when the house and the light will again emerge.

EMERGEMCE
Vicki

Spring is a wonderful season with the emergence of new life after so long being asleep. Daffodils – Primroses – Crocuses – are first to appear. All with their abundance of colours. Then Tulips and Lily of the Valley making everywhere bright and cheery, after dull dark and cold months. Watching the new leaves uncurl on branches of the trees and hedges is a delight. To stand and look at all the creatures getting excited with such glory of all the wild life starting to wake up – taking in all the new surroundings of such splendour of worms, larvae, hazel nuts, caterpillars, beetles, insects.

Spring brings the migrating birds back to our shores. What an amazing sight to see all breeds of birds flying overhead, waiting to take their place in the lakes or marshes.

Spring is alive with Song-thrush, Nightingales, Blackbirds, Robins singing choruses to each other. We know Spring is here.

CLARA'S STORY
Margaret

Clara sat drinking her tea and gazing out of the window. She decided she would make the most of the sunshine and steady weather. She was a woman of her word. Before she knew it, she'd booked a taxi to take her to a craft show a short distance away. She was an artist and craft worker.

She arrived at the venue and walked in. Instantly, a good feeling enveloped her. So much talent around. It was true. The stall holders were her friends from over the years of working together. Having had a good chat and catch up, it was time to go home. She decided she would spend some time in the park to make the most of the beautiful day.

Stepping outside after the goodbyes with her friends, she paused for a while. How long had it been since she had done a good walk? Too long. So, she set off, having decided to walk the long way home. What a delight. Every moment she could see changes and improvements around her. She relished the joy of the birds and the flowers and trees, In fact, nature in general. Heaven!

She wasn't rushing. There was no hurry. After all, she was retired and had recovered from major illness and trauma. Such freedom, such an adventure. Passing people smiled at her as if they knew what pleasure she was feeling. It must have been a stroll of about three miles, through parks and roadways and byways. How fit she felt.

"Maybe I can do a bit of shopping at Tesco," she thought. "Well, why not?"

The pride she felt in her achievement was undeniable. She reached home and sat down, astounded by the joyous way the day went. For now, she would have a nap and wake up with plans to do more of the same, - later! In fact, another day. Recovery first. She smiled a contented smile to herself. What a life!

After awhile the wood seemed to settle down and I opened my eyes. The ground surrounding me had turned from green to blue and white as if by magic. When I had arrived an hour or so earlier the heads of the bluebells and wood anemones were drooping in the cool of the night and had gone unnoticed. Now I couldn't believe my eyes. As I looked around me, all I could see was a carpet of blue with the white stars of the wood anemones peeping in between. The flowers appeared to be dancing between the shadows and the sunbeams.

What a wonderful morning. I felt alive with the miracle of it all. The birds had quietened down now and the beginnings of the day could be heard from the vehicles on the nearby road. People were journeying to work and school. Ah well, back to normal for another day.

CHAPTER SEVEN
DESCRIPTIVE WRITING

BLODWYN EVANS – HOUSEWIFE
Keith

Blodwyn is a very elderly Welsh lady. Her home is in Llandudno, North Wales. You will see her about town and even takes the bus to Conwy where she used to show visitors the smallest house in Great Britain on the quay in Conwy.

Now her once 6' height is stooped with arthritis and she walks with the aid of two walking sticks. Her hair is pure white. Her eyes behind dark glasses are turquoise blue. Her skin care-worn and dark. Her voice is very quiet, as quiet as her breath.

Despite her age and feebleness, she maintains a smile for everyone she meets. All her family have either died or left home. Her appointed carers call on her at least once a day as she doggedly holds on to her independence in "her home".

"You will have to take me out in a box," she

declares to all who want her to go in a care home. "This is my family home. I want to die here!"

She had moved in on her wedding day over 50 years ago, had brought up four children and helped them create families of their own. Now they had all moved away.

Her husband David, a housebuilder, had also moved on to what she called "his heavenly home". She now waited to join him there.

JOE BRIGGS
Anna

Joe (John) Briggs was born in the early 1900s in Durham. He was the fifth boy in a miner's family, an afterthought ten years after the youngest boy. They lived in a solid three-bed house about half a mile from the coal mine, had a good veg garden and flowers with a comfortable wage coming in, had plenty of food, serviceable clothes, and boots, with plenty of free coal.

His father and mother were Chapel people, but not too rigid, so his father was allowed a good pint of ale on a Saturday night and the older boys when old enough. His mother was a calm, homely lady. It was a very close, loving family. Joe went to the local school and did well, but was expected to go into the mines when old enough, which he did when he was about fourteen where he initially looked after the pit ponies hauling the tubs of coal. A kind boy, he loved this job. By now he was a handsome young man. He had a thick shock of untidy black hair, always blowing everywhere, the bluest of eyes. Long-lashed as any girl. He was about 5 feet. Stocky, muscular, and very fit. In his spare time, he loved fell running with the local team and made every opportunity to get out in the fresh air and observe nature, go fishing and generally unwind.

Joe grew into a very kind and honest man, ready to help anyone if he could. There were many widows, old people, and children in the village. Some in dire straits with no man to help them. Joe did what he could, as did his whole family as they had more to give. He also had a good sense of humour and was also the comedian in any village plays or events. His round face never serious and always cheering up anyone he met. He, along with his family, enjoyed sharing Chapel on Sundays and on other occasions. All boys and the father were in the choir and Joe, being talented at the Reed organ which he had self-taught.

The minister had been a miner so knew how people here felt and was on their level. The village was a real caring community. Picnics were enjoyed, an annual charabanc outing and events through the year.

Joe was a star in the pantomime as the young man or Dame. He dressed very smartly when going out. Good classic fashion. Breaches, long socks, a snow-white shirt, a very colourful waistcoat and the shiniest of black, calfskin boots. In winter he had a thick tweed cape coat.

He was pleasant with the girls but no sweetheart yet. Later he fell in love with a lovely pretty girl who was a maid in the big house. She had a disposition like Joe and they made a solid couple, going on to have a house and three children.

As a grown man, Joe was a full miner. Although dangerous, dirty work, he enjoyed the comradeship. The mine owners were extremely caring of the men, providing hot showers and medical aid for injuries. No one lost money if they had to go sick. A scheme of 2p a week was paid in which gathered a little interest. It helped in times of sickness. And help was given in practical ways if anyone was killed or unable to work. The best mine around. So, the miners were a happy bunch and repaid the good conditions by working harder.

Joe was now in his 60's, still happily married, rather portly but fit. His family had grown and moved away from the mining area, but still were very close-knit. Joe was slowing up and working above the mine in management. His shock of hair now white, but a handsome, kindly man helping and listening to anyone needing him.

His wife made soup and some food for those ill or out of work with a team of ladies. Life was placid and good.

Next year. Joe will retire from the mine, but will never step into idleness. He can just ease up and enjoy his freedom. Maybe grow more vegetables, keep a few more chickens, and enjoy his new hobby of pigeon racing. A well-deserved easement of life.

SHALL WE DANCE?
Vicki

I was invited to my cousins 60th birthday and was glad I decided to go instead of making an excuse not to. Over the years I've been to many parties of some sort and never stayed longer than necessary. All these do's never appealed to me. They were all noisy and dark with flashing lights. Music so loud you couldn't hear conversation and had to shout to be heard.

More often than not, I would find a corner tucked away from all the racket. I'd sit quietly watching everyone making fools of themselves with contortionist dance movements, some even falling over. It's amazing what too much drink can do. I must admit though, some of the antics did make me smile.

This birthday party wasn't anything like the ones I had been to before. There was no loud music and flashing lights in a dark room. This was at her house in the afternoon with open windows and the patio door leading to the garden with a marquee. There was buntings and balloons all around the garden, music played by a quartet of drums, two guitars, a saxophone and keyboard.

The buffet was in the kitchen with the use of a microwave if you wanted a warm any of the food like pizzas, sausage rolls or Cornish pasties. The buffet was overwhelming with such a spread and the choice of so many different dishes.

The quarter played old songs of the 50s, 60's, 70s, 90's, and not leaving the youngsters out, the 'Naughties' which sounded alien to me.

I sat under a tree for shade from the sun, with a drink and sandwich, enjoying the atmosphere of the day, when a voice by my side said, "Shall we dance? You look as though you really want to, and here I am to partner you. Besides, you're the best-looking woman here!" He was my cousin's uncle, handsome for his age, dressed in a blue blazer, white polo-necked T-shirt, pale blue trousers, and white moccasin style shoes. "How could I refuse?"

MARY DAWSON-BLIGH
Dee

Mary stepped out of her BMW onto the gravel drive, not noticing how her high heels sank between the stones. Leaving the door wide open, she walked towards the house. Reaching the front door, she turned and glanced back at the long driveway. All seemed as it should be. The wrought iron security gates were just closing.

She swivelled back to the front door that looked as it usually did, but something was wrong. Mary couldn't work out what it was. As she leaned forward to insert the key, the door mysteriously opened. That shouldn't have happened. She was sure she had locked it when she went out that morning.

Where had she been that morning? It was all a blur as she passed the ornate hall mirror. She stopped to face her reflection. Her beautifully quaffed blonde hair was in place. No need to pat it, but out of habit she ran her hand along the waves. Around her neck was her favourite Hermes silk scarf, hiding the lines that were now tracing their way around her throat. Not bad for my age, she mused. She leaned in closer and realised that her red lipstick needed repairing. She'd see to it later.

Moving along the wide hall, she heard a noise coming from the kitchen and a voice called out, "Afternoon, Mrs Dawson-Bligh. I've got the kettle on. I'll make you a nice cup of tea. Expect you'll need it after this morning. How did it go?"

Mary blinked and inhaled.

"Fine, thank you." She didn't really feel like

having a cup of tea, especially not wanting to sit and talk while desperately trying to remember what she had been doing that morning. Why did she need a cup of tea?

She decided to go upstairs to her office. Maybe that will give her some clues, but why couldn't she remember? The familiar surroundings and furniture in her office gave her some comfort. There was her ergonomic office chair, her computer, and the paraphernalia of her life. A photograph stood on the state-of-the-art desk, showing her linking arms with a handsome elderly man. She picked the frame up and sighed. Now, this man she definitely remembered. Good old Frank, her husband of 45 years who had passed away two years previously. "Well, that's a relief," she thought. "At least I know who that is."

The office chair looked inviting. She always loved to sit and look out of the large sash window at the fabulous sight of the flower beds and lawns that lead to a spectacular view of the river. Still puzzling over the morning's mysterious event, she leant back and closed her eyes.

A vision came into her mind of a crowded room full of men and women in office attire. They were strangers to her, but everyone was congratulating her, smiling, and wanting to shake her hand. Some were even hugging and air-kissing her. It was most embarrassing. Who were they all, and what had she done to be praised? A woman stood on a podium and began making a speech. It was about a person who was now retiring but had spent their career working tirelessly to help pass legislation that would protect vulnerable young people. The speech went on and on, interspersed with applause when the crowd turned towards Mary. As the woman made her closing sentence, A man hopped rather elegantly onto the podium. Mary's eyes became glued to the man. This was finally someone she knew. She made her way towards him, rudely pushing people aside. She was followed by mutterings and tuts, but regardless of it all, she soon reached the man and slipped her hand around his waist. With her other hand, she caressed his cheek. Oh, so familiar. She could feel his breath on her forehead as she leaned against his chest. This was how she remembered him holding her close skin on skin as he stroked her hair. He always told her how he loved her soft curves, but they had never been able to show their feelings outside. She'd always been perfectly discreet, knowing she would never be his wife or have his children. That's why she had worked with disadvantaged kids as compensation. Suddenly rough hands grabbed her by the shoulders and dragged her away from the room.

    Back in her office Mary sat bolt upright, then flung herself forward, head in hands. It all came flooding back to her. She was the one who was retiring, had worked tirelessly throughout her career. The gathering and speech were in her honour. She was remembering in stomach-churning clarity. She was retiring because of her memory losses; her working life was no longer viable. Now with one lapse of memory she had ruined everything, almost certainly wrecking her lover's career and marriage. Her secret was out. Their secret was out.

WIZARDS
Anna

They lived in large caves and wore a long robe made from woven lambs-wool, dyed with natural colour. They grew their hair and beards long, but no one feared them. They collected all kinds of herbs, berries, and leaves for their medicine supply and ate only what they gathered or on the little gifts of vegetables and maybe small pieces of meat taken in exchange for help and healing.

PC FREDDIE SCOTT
Myrtle

Archie Brown slouched back on the hard wooden chair on the wrong side of the table in Interview Room B and regarded PC Freddie Scott through insolent eyes. He hadn't seen this copper before today, and he reckoned he could tie him up in knots, no trouble. PC Freddie Scott regarded him steadily back. Scott knew he looked like a soft touch and used the fact to its full advantage. Relaxed villains tended to drop their guard and reveal more than they intended. Heading for his 30th birthday, Scott looked closer to 20 with his bleach-blonde hair and baby-blue eyes. Those eyes, set in a clean-shaven face with a hint of a dimple in his left cheek, gave him an air of innocence that was far from the truth. His tan owed more to the salon than to holidays abroad and he kept his lean 6ft 2in frame perfectly in trim by lunchtime visits to the gym. Scott was clearly a man who cared deeply about his appearance. He didn't even look like a flat-footed copper, Archie decided. More like some namby-pamby model in his immaculate uniform.

OK, so he could run fast, he'd give the guy that. That's how he got him in here after that car job. But he didn't look as though there was much going on in that pretty head of his. Archie's contemptuous gaze took in the perfectly clean, manicured nails and the long slender fingers resting lightly on the table opposite him. Yeah, soft touch for sure.

Scott listened as DI Craddock continued the interview. He had trained himself to sit perfectly still, his head slightly inclined towards the DI, as though in deference to his immediate boss. It paid to show deference he had learnt. In truth, he knew that he was in every way superior to the man and that eventually the promotions he deserved would take him way beyond DI Craddock's team. Ambition drove him. There was little time for relationships. There was the occasional hook- up with some guy he'd met at the gym or had a drink with at the wine bar in a neighbouring town. All very discreet, of course, nothing permanent. He spent most of his evenings home alone. He would change into his joggers and vest to pull a few weights or put in a half hour of rowing in his home gym before cooking a light supper, maybe a stir fry or a veggie curry. He would spend an hour or two reviewing old cases, studying the methods that had led to arrests and successful prosecutions. On Saturdays, he would put in as many extra hours as were necessary to keep his current paperwork in meticulous order. Sundays were reserved for visits to his mother, who lived in Redman King House in the seaside town of Eastbourne, although a large part of the day would be taken up by the opportunity for a serious swim in the waves of the English Channel. Yes, PC Freddie Scott was definitely going places.

VICTOR STARR
Margaret

As she walked up the steps of the Catholic Church in Pinner, North London, she realised she would be saying a very final goodbye to the finest man she'd ever known. This memorial was a tribute to one of the last of a kind. She was quietly shown to her seat in the front row by a very sympathetic usher. She sat peacefully recalling every detail of everything she'd ever known about Victor Star, perhaps the last real entrepreneur of this century.

She pondered on the fact that he was fair-haired, unlike most of his kind, they always seem to be dark-haired. She smiled to herself at the thought. He was, of course, fair in colouring in every way. His blue eyes seemed to have the ability to show how happy he was by nature. He was a very tall man and therefore radiated an extremely confident personality. Definitely, a man, completely reliable, trustworthy and of strong character. She also remembered him for being very fit, extremely healthy. His lifestyle encompassed all his great wealth could provide. He'd always been a very smart man, always the best men's stores and styles. He really could have won 'Man of the Year', and in every sense.

Of course, when she first met him, it was the time before he made his, shall we say, 'Empire'. Thank goodness he used all he made of his wealth to help others. His own lifestyle was quite steady really. He liked gardening, tennis etc and had many, many hobbies, interests including the welfare of the less fortunate and young people looking for a better future. He constantly worked towards helping others, also upcoming small businesses. Companies as well. Most of his wealth went towards other people, maybe for tax purposes for all she knew.

She had always respected his amazingly strong personality and character because his kindness overruled it all. She was so glad she had known such a man who was also a strong family-minded man. He liked to see people challenged but happy in their work, also their life. She remembered his home as being expensive, but in its way, simple. Yes, it had a swimming pool and tennis court and gym. Then again, he let it out to the small groups of young or less fortunate kids for use on one day a week. For free! Overseen by one of his trusted, loyal members of staff. Always arranged for when he had a day out with his family.

Some people wondered where his money came from. While his start in life was a simple one, he had known suffering. His mother, a lovely lady, died much too young. He was very much a self-made man with a good degree of ambition. This, however, never changed his belief in trying for a better world. Oh, how he would be missed for the man he was. She came with a start back from her thoughts to the memorial.

COLOURS
Lorna

Tan shoes and pink shoelaces for walking on the white lines painted on the road. "There's a song somewhere in there," the traffic warden said as the dandy tap-danced on the kerb stones, balancing like a ballet dancer as he wove his way along the Main Street. His polka dot hat sat at a jaunty angle on his jet-black hair. Sparkling brown eyes and an apricot-coloured bow tie completed his outfit. He was a sight to gladden the heart of any maiden.

THE ROYAL FUNERAL
Dee

The hearse carrying the Queen's coffin, entirely alone now, bereft of the cortege came to a standstill on the lonely country road. No crowds here, only green fields and hedgerows. A handful of people stood at the gates of their front gardens in silence.

The car moved slowly forward until it reached two columns of red-coated soldiers standing to attention on either side of the narrow road. Their tall bearskin hats towered over the hearse. As one, they began to march slowly and majestically forward, almost seeming to carry the vehicle.

In the distance was the swelling sound of the pipers as they played the Skye Boat song. Then the sound of the pipes was exchanged for the music of the band of the Dismounted Cavalry, along with the incessant beat of the drum. A jangle of metal grew louder as many of the Queens Mounted Household Cavalry turned from a side road to join the procession.

Armed police stalked the verges, keeping a watchful eye across the hedges to the fields beyond.

An incredible sight met our eyes as the procession neared the Windsor Long Walk. Swathes of flowers had been laid beside the road. Still no crowds, but in the distance were once again the people who had come out to wish our Sovereign blessings on her final journey. Even her favourite pony, Emma and two Corgis stood to attention as she passed by.

Bravo to the many, many boys and girls, men, and women, who had given their all in such a respectful and dignified way to mark this sombre occasion.

And bravo to King Charles and all the royal family who braved such a difficult time in the face of the whole world. I say God bless them.

THE DEATH OF OUR QUEEN ELIZABETH 11
Anna

My first emotion on hearing of her sudden death was one of great sadness, yet glad that she can at last be free and have a rest. Can you imagine working full time with a few days off for seventy years? It brought back strong feelings for those loved ones I have lost. Like losing my son, my dear grandmother, aunts, and others that I have loved.

She was the mother of England and many countries around the globe. A selfless, caring, dignified and beautiful woman outside and within, and with a good sense of humour. Neither arrogant nor prejudiced. Her life was not easy, having family and personal problems like everyone. She had so little time to escape to her beloved Balmoral in which to unwind and have fun with her family. She always had to be dressed up on show. No curling up in an old skirt and slippers. She did her duty until she died, keeping all her coronation vows. She is still on public view in her coffin. But soon she will be able to clock off permanently and enjoy eternal peace and rest with her loved ones. God bless and thank you, Ma'am. RIP.

THOUGHTS ON THE QUEEN
Vicki

Thinking about the Queen as I often did over the years of her long reign. She never once wanted to be Queen. Her life was like an open prison. She could go anywhere in the world, but always bodyguards, police, and protection every place she went to visit.

I often thought how lovely to be free. Nip down the local pub or local shop without being escorted. It would have been heaven when the Queen had her time off for holidays and such. To be able to relax and let her hair down away from the public eye. She was quite funny and a mimic from what come-back we get from presenters and close friends and family. How the Queen must have loved those short breaks to be with her family. No, I wouldn't have wanted her job, not for a billion pounds. God rest her soul and look after her in heaven.

A MYSTICAL PLACE
Anna

I am going to take you into a magical and beautiful world that existed in days of yore. The world was much smaller. The countryside spread far and wide with few habitations, only small villages, and scattered cottages. No towns. The land was divided up into Wizdoms, governed by Wizards. These were very wise and caring men. The people grew all the fruit and vegetables they needed, kept cows, goats, pigs, and chickens, but not too many, sufficient for their needs and a little extra. Money was unknown as people bartered anything to spare.

All lived in caring, peaceful harmony. If anyone needed healing, they visited the wizard who recommended herbs or other simple remedies, but that was a rare occasion.

Tucked away quietly but living with the big people were the fairies and dwarves in barns, empty rabbit holes, holes in trees or in their roots, they could be found. But the fairies only worked at night, secretly. Houses were never locked, so they could easily enter. They would polish the stove, wash the eggs, sweep the hearth and other small chores to help the busy housewife. Also take away the children's teeth left under pillows in exchange for a flower or pretty stone.

The dwarves worked in the tin and copper mines for tools and utensils and to collect clay for pots and bricks. They did other jobs like chopping wood, grooming a horse, polishing the goats' feet, weeding and other useful things, all at night too.

On Midsummer's night, the big people had their feast and danced around a bonfire.

The little people had their own with delicious bat-saliva and honey wine, spring-water cordial and to eat, Sooty Berry tarts, pies of tiny fish and a special stew of barley, green turnips, carrots, minced beef mushrooms and herbs like Sparsley and Beau Brummel leaves. They sat on low mushroom stools around a cluster of glittering moon drops and sang and danced daintily.

The dwarves had their own party but wore clogs and drank beer from acorn cups, made from brewed nettles and hyssop and got very merry.

That was long ago. The land eventually was washed away by the sea. But there are still some little people to be found, if you know where to look. If you have lost something, make a wish to a fairy and maybe it will appear the next day, or its whereabouts will be whispered in your ear when you are asleep. If riding in a car at night, you might see some tiny shapes flying in the headlights. No, they are not insects. They are fairies flying out to do their tasks. Remember to leave a saucer of milk for them. The dwarves too are around, but not so many as machines do a lot of the work for them. They still leave a basket of wood by the doorstep, scare the fox from the hen coop, gather rabbit and sheep fur for their beds.

As you walk along, glance in tree roots, nooks, and crannies, but don't touch. It maybe someone's home. Have respect for the flowers and berries in the hedgerows, they may be a little person's garden. Just let your imagination expand Because we cannot see everything, it doesn't mean it doesn't exist.

CHAPTER EIGHT
TONGUE TWISTERS

From the Group

Several salmon swam the seas, which brought the fisherman to his knees.

Sadly, Medly made a plan, which did upset her miserable man.

The snowman came, the snowman went and melted in the fox's tent.

The sea sinks the ship when the ship springs a leak.

Fred Flint flings the flint in the axe the first time.

My sister went to a fiesta and my sister saw a sister at the fiesta in her vesta.

Poppy potted potato pots.

The party pooper pulled his party popper properly.

Fifty fat Frenchmen fried fish and frog fingers for finest females.

Twenty-two new tools twang in tune.

Black-heads bled red blood back and blue blooming banging boomerangs

Strict stitchers stitched switchers for witches.

Intense incense sent innocents and gents in tents.

The train to Totness Tooted Toot Toot.

We went to Wales in waterproof Wellingtons.

Chester chose a cheese and chutney sandwich.

Faster, faster fled the filly far across the field.

Snip, snap, slap, slip, went the silver sails.

CHAPTER NINE
DIALOGUE

THE PROPOSAL
Myrtle

"I'll send a car at 7,' you said. 'To get you to the Strand Hotel at 7:30. I'll be there straight from work., you said" I look at Clive accusingly as he takes his seat opposite me at the table.

"I'm sorry, darling, just a last-minute hold-up. So, you did wear the red dress after all! This is such a special Valentine's Day. You look amazing!"

"You're changing the subject, Clive. I've been waiting for..."

Clive interrupts. "I know, darling, I'm so sorry. You've waited for so long and you're cross with me." His tone was placatory. "But don't let's spoil our evening."

"Yes," my mind replies. "I've waited too long. Ten long years for your children to finish their schooling. Then your wife's cancer, when you couldn't possibly leave her." But all I actually said was, "Half an hour, Clive. I was beginning to think you'd changed your mind."

I didn't tell him either about the elderly woman in the bay window opposite and her overheard whisper. "Do you think she's been stood up?" Or that other woman's not-so-subtle glance and the words I wasn't sure if I'd misheard, "Red... complexion...tarty."

"And besides," I say to Clive, "I look better in the blue."

"Sweetheart, you look wonderful in anything." He lowers his voice and leans in across the table. "And even better in nothing." I don't reply, so Clive ploughs on. "I've asked the waiter to put some champagne on ice. Let's put this behind us, sweetheart." As if a few bubbles will blot out the long wait. So, I smile and try to play along. I know what this is leading up to.

"What have you..." I begin as Clive produces a tiny box from his jacket pocket.

"Darling, I told you this is a special Valentine's Day." He opens the box and I gasp at the glittering rock it contains. "How beautiful," I murmur. "How expensive," I think.

"Darling, will you marry me?"

Half an hour ago, I would have said, "yes."

I look up into his eyes. "No, Clive," I say. "It's too late."

THE WAITING GAME
Dee

For the umpteenth time, she looked at her watch and sighed. They'd agreed to meet in the park at 2pm. A quarter past and still no sign of him or his car. She had to admit to herself that they hadn't actually specified where they would meet, but surely, he would know that she would go through the gate that was nearest to the direction she would arrive. Surely the road he would take, would be the one directly opposite that entrance. It all made perfect sense to her.

"Why was it that when it came to doing something with her, he was always late, whereas when they were going to a concert or other event of his choosing, he wanted to be extra early?"

She decided to get out of the car and have a little wander, keeping an eye on the road in case he should drive by. The park was very disappointing, which didn't help her mood that was now descending into black. Litter was strewn around the bins, so she didn't want to venture anywhere near them. She forced herself not to look at her watch. But took out her mobile. No signal.

"That means we can't contact one another," she thought.

As she sat down on the very edge of a not particularly inviting bench on the banks of the lake, she tried to find something to enjoy, to lift her spirits. To her horror, she realised she was staring at a rat that was rummaging through the undergrowth beside the water's edge not six feet away from her. Quickly rising to her feet and anxiously glancing round, she scurried back to the car.

He was now twenty-five minutes late according to her calculations, but to give him the benefit of the doubt, she thought she should drive through the park to the further entrance past the cafe. She reached all the way to the end without a glimpse of his car or him.

"This is beyond acceptable now," she fumed to herself. Reaching her starting point, she decided to give him another fifteen minutes. Still no signal on her mobile.

"Even if he thought we were meeting at 2:30 he is still late. He just doesn't listen anymore. We used to be on the same wavelength, knowing what the other was thinking, enjoying the same things. But lately we seem to have lost that connection."

All these thoughts were turning around in her brain.

"I don't want to do this anymore," she finally concluded. "If he can't be bothered to be on time for me. I'm off. I'm not playing the waiting game anymore."

She started the engine and with a final glance in the rear-view mirror, drove home.

BOYS WILL BE BOYS
Margaret

As Sarah stood gazing out of her kitchen window whilst washing up, there was a knock on her front door. She was flummoxed as to what it could be about. It was Mabel from next door.

Mabel said, "Here, Sarah, there's a hell of a hullabaloo out in the street. Real shenanigans. Your young whippersnapper is with the scallywag from round the corner."

"Quite a malarkey then," replied Sarah. "I hope with most boys being rapscallions that the ragamuffin, what's his name?"

"He's Ned," said Mabel.

"He's a bit of a nincompoop, capable of bamboozling your Joey into bother. Especially if he's got his football with him. His mate broke a window last week, then he'll get out of it. Blame who he's with."

"A right tarradiddle. He's bound to bring some sort of gubbins or maybe the thingamajig we saw him win at the fair last weekend. That looked awful."

"That could be a tarradiddle, of course. You know how it is these days."

"OK, thanks for letting me know," Sarah replied. "There's no peace for the wicked, is there? May see you later if worse ensues."

Back to the washing up also the rest of her household chores. Life was better for her in these times. Many were far worse off. She knew one day things would improve but didn't realise it would take a World War to achieve it. The women may get the vote, then the voices of change would be heard. Maybe she would join the group of women. She'd heard some of them talking about it. Who knows? Just now she had work to do.

THE MEETING
Vicki

He sat on the bench in the railway station. There were a few people lingering around, waiting for their train. Over the intercom, the announcer said, "Runnymede, Belshaw. Dillingen and Harmsway will arrive on time. Change at Tweetford for Godling."

Simon made himself as comfortable as possible on the hard seat and took out his paper to settle down to wait for the train, which made him nervous thinking about how he will greet Diane as she departs from the train.

Diane was a young lady he used to see in the bank when she came in to pay her company's money in their account. Many times, for the last couple of months, Simon wanted to ask her out but never had the courage. Then one day, he decided it was now or never. He went over to her in the queue, a bit shaky with nerves.

"I'm Simon and have seen you every week for months. I wanted to ask you out for a drink but never had the courage till now. I would be honoured if you said you would."

The young lady with beautiful brown eyes and chestnut colour hair was quiet. She was quite surprised, so Simon was embarrassed.

But then she said. "I'm Diane. I would love to have a drink with you."

Seeing his vacant look turn into the most sparkling smile made her notice how his face softened, making him rather handsome in a way. His light brown curly hair and deep Hazel eyes were mesmerising.

Waiting on the platform was interesting. So many people going to their day-to-day routines. He wondered where they were going, where they came from and what kind of life they lived. That brought him to think of Diane. All he knew about her was her name, Diane. She was an accountant, which meant they must be right for each other as he was an accountant for the bank.

The train was nearly due and Simon started to get fidgety. They said they would meet at 7 o'clock. He'd got there fifteen minutes early to get himself calm for the meeting. When the train arrived on time, Simon started to walk along the platform to see if he could see her. One by one the passengers dwindled until there were no passengers at all and the train pulled away.

Simon was so disappointed that he sat down on the hard bench and thought of what could have been the reason for not turning up.

Could she have changed her mind and realised he wasn't up to her standards? Perhaps being an accountant like her, makes her feel threatened. What if she's had an accident on her way? That would be so cruel. Suppose she was on her way and got off the train a stop before 'cause she changed her mind at the last minute. Perhaps she missed the train and will catch the next one.

Simon couldn't help himself from thinking what might have been. He decided he would wait for the next train, as he had already waited 45 minutes or more. Not including the 15 minutes he was early. He could not accept she would stand him up on purpose. Diane didn't seem to be a girl who would do that.

After a further 20 minutes, the announcer said over a crackling intercom, "The train from Runnymead to Harmsway will arrive on time and the journey will end at Harmsway.

Simon was more nervous than ever waiting for the train and was pacing up and down. When the train did arrive, he stayed glued to the spot, hoping Diane would be would be walking on the platform.

As the passengers thinned out, he saw her walking in between two people looking at her watch, trying to walk a faster pace.

When he saw her, he was blown away with her beauty. She was wearing her hair down. It had always been tied back in a bun. Her white blouse glittered with red dots. A red skirt above her knees. She always wore Navy. Navy jacket with her skirt to her shins. Red shoes with high heels, always Navy shoes with Cuban heels to go with the uniform and a red envelope bag.

She looked stunning and Simon was fixed to the

spot, just gazing at her. Love was overflowing and his heart was pounding.

As soon as Diane saw him, she ran straight towards him, arms outstretched, flinging her arms around his neck she kissed him on his lips.

Pulling away, she said, "Oh Simon, I am so sorry. I missed the train. It was my sister's fault. She was supposed to pick Peter up and she was late.

Simon sighed quietly when he heard the name Peter. Was that her son?

Then Diane went on to say, "I was so mad at my sister. She said she would be back in plenty of time. Otherwise, I would never have volunteered to look after my nephew. I nearly never turned up as it was so late and I thought you would have gone. I'm so happy you never did and took a chance to wait. Thank you. Mr Simon, who is looking so dapper in his Navy suit and pale blue shirt and Navy tie. I'm so delighted to be your date with such a handsome escort."

BETTY BRIGHT
Lorna

I was walking along 5th Ave, my bag over my arm. I'd been in to buy a new hat, something stylish but different. I became aware of someone's chirpy voice calling, "Betty? Betty Bright?" But I wasn't paying attention because my thoughts were all focused on the new song and dance, we were rehearsing. I knew the lyrics pretty well and my solo part, but it's always the dance steps that take a bit longer to memorise.

Of course, Niki always has a charming word to say when I trip up. It's just that my memory keeps fading and I have to improvise, like the time we were doing the Cygnets dance from Swan Lake for the Queen and Prince Philip. The old king had died recently and they both sat there in the royal box with sad faces. He looked thoroughly bored. It was the part where the two rows go in opposite directions. Maestro had warned us not to make a mistake on pain of death or worse. I was watching the Queen's face, so sad. I wondered if Swan Lake had been a favourite of the old king. Of course, the worst thing happened. I only went and turned the wrong way and upset the two rows which brought a frown to the prince's face. But the Queen hid her laugh in her handkerchief. Maestro said he would forgive me, since it made the Queen smile.

"Fanny," I heard somewhere in the crowds walking about the pavement, I turned to see who could be calling me.

"Come on, Fanny, you Remember Me?" It was one of the girls. "Golden Gladys," I exclaimed.

"Yes, you silly thing. Where were you? Away in Memory Lane." Well, yes, I was. I looked at her. Her real name was Mary Brown. Golden Gladys was the stage name we used when we sang as a duo. I was Silver Sylvie; contralto and she was mezzo soprano. Those were great days.

"I was calling you, Sylvie," she said looking into my eyes, "You haven't changed a bit. Still such wonderful white hair and your green eyes. The men fell in droves at your feet."

"I think the boots on the other foot, or should I say the ballet pointes." She still had glorious auburn hair, still worn in sumptuous waves on top of her head.

"I love your outfit, Syl."

It was something new. A soft silky material in taupe, black and white. Very simple, very elegant. My coat was bespoke and covered me like a hug. It was so comfortable. I wore sensible black patent leather shoes and handbag to match. The shoes alone had been £400 but were so comfortable I didn't feel the least bit guilty. My black Pearl earrings and necklace were a present.

"Let's pop into Concerto. It's a new restaurant."

We had wandered up to the entrance. As we stood at the door, we were reflected in its glass. Two tall, elegant women. One blonde, the other burnished copper. We had always stood together in the lineup. The shorter girls graded away from tallest to smallest, emphasising us. We stood out. We stood tall. We looked at each other and smiled. Green eyes and cornflower blue.

We sat at a table near the back with a view of everyone in the room. We placed our orders.

"I'll have a pomegranate tea, please," said Gladys, turning to Betty with an enquiring mind smile.

"And for you, ma'am?" The Italian-looking waiter said, pen poised.

"He has the most deliciously deep, sexy voice, don't you think?" Said Gladys in a whisper behind her hand, peeping up at him.

He smiled self-consciously, but kept his dark eyes on Betty. "Thank you," she said, pausing while she had a little conversation with herself.

"I really want a coffee and one of those limoncello cakes, but if she's only having a fruit tea, I suppose she's looking after her figure. I wonder if she's still dancing? Bit old for that now, surely? What, Dear? I suddenly realised that two pairs of eyes were watching me.

"Oh dear, did I say that out loud?"

"No, Ma'am," said the waiter. His badge said he

was Diego. "You were about to order." He smiled brilliantly.

"I'd love a cup of Duke of Wellington and Limoncello cake." I looked up into his dark eyes, deep as wells.

"I wonder if they're brown or black," I thought.

"Pardon Ma'am? Gladys gave a little squeak and quickly hid her face with a lace hanky. Her eyes were sparkling.

"Oh dear, have I said something rude?" I looked from one to the other.

"No Ma'am, but I think you would like Earl Grey tea?"

"Yes, of course I would." I smiled happily at him.

"You're so clever. That's exactly what I would like too. And the limoncello cake. Don't forget?" Gladys smiled.

He bowed and walked quickly away, his shoulders quaking with suppressed laughter.

A STORY OF HOPE IN TROUBLED TIMES
Margaret

The shops were lighting up now as Marjorie decided to curtail her walk and head for home. She enjoyed her time with her friends pursuing their hobbies. As she passed the store, she was struck by the sight of a beautiful blanket draped over the chair. The setting was definitely Middle-Eastern. The Persians have always been so artistic.

Her friend was finally coming into view. She wanted to make sure Angie saw the blanket, so when she arrived, she drew her attention to the shop window.

"Look at that beautiful blanket," she said.

Oh yes," said her friend, Angie. "Marjorie, that is gorgeous. Look at those colours."

Marjorie straight away said, "That's an Afghan blanket, you know. I've seen them before, but this one is spectacular. They say another lot of refugees have come in and we're going to accept twenty of them. Every thread of that blanket tells a story of human suffering."

"Yes," said Angie. "Our lives are blessed. The setting that they have placed it then looks so authentic with the draped shawl and other effects."

Marjorie said, "I understand they're holding a special dinner and dance and will sell that blanket to raise funds for the incomers. Thousands of pounds will be raised, then so much more can be done to help these poor, unfortunate people in their time of such suffering and need. They're moving this arrangement to a corner of the hall they're using for the fundraiser. My friend Sally is going with her husband, so I'll find out quite soon how much they raise,"

"I'm amazed at the amount of work that's gone into this blanket. When you think about every line and colour denotes a family suffering. The colours are of their past history.

It's an inspiration to us all."

Marjorie felt so overwhelmed by the emotion that looking at the blanket brought about in her, that it stirred something in her long since buried, something that seemed to want to be heard and perhaps could not be said. Suffering was not alien to her. As with most people, it was part of her life. Oh, how glad she was that she had overcome such dark times and moved on in life to become a woman of understanding, had become the well-rounded and grounded woman that she was.

THE AUDITION
Lorna

It was early evening, a week after her first appointment. A little smile tipped the corners of her mouth up and her eyes sparkled. She was wearing her new dress, a cornflower blue that matched her eyes and complemented her Auburn hair. She dabbed a drop or two of perfume onto her neck where she could feel a strong, steady pulse. She was ready.

As she came downstairs, her sister stepped out of her room. "Wow, you look stunning," exclaimed Patsy.

"Thank you," Jenny murmured with a little tip of her head.

"What's going on?" That was Jerry who came out of his room to look.

"Pooh, you smell," he said with a cheeky look on his face.

"My goodness, Jen!" Her mother's voice was breathless as she turned back to the sitting room.

"Jim, come and see," she said, flapping her hand to make him hurry. Jim's black-rimmed glasses were on the tip of his nose and he pushed them back, then took them off to wipe them on his shirt, and put them on again and peer through them with his head tipped back.

"Jim, stop fooling around," said mum.

"I was just wondering who that is," he said

innocently, a proud smile on his face. "You look lovely."

"Thank you." Jenny felt herself blushing. This was a happy moment for her, and she glowed in her family's approval.

"Taxi's here," roared Jerry, coming down the last few steps and rushing to open the door. He nearly missed the vase of flowers on the hall table, but caught it as it began to tumble and placed it back in its place with a guilty look over his shoulder.

"Sorry, Mum," he blurted and sprang to open the door.

"Have you got a hanky, dear?"

"Yes, Mum."

"Keys?"

"Yes, Dad."

Patsy pushed something into her hand.

"In case you need a mouth freshener," she whispered as she slipped the little spray bottle into Jenny's bag.

Sitting in the taxi, Jenny thought about the events of the past week, her interview with the director, producer, choreographer, and casting director. She was nervous before she went in, sitting with several other people. But once the wait was over, she began to feel sure that she would get the part and as she stepped onto the stage, she was filled with self-confidence and a premonition that her time had come.

REBEKAH AND HENRY IN RETIREMENT
Anna

Rebekah had just retired at sixty from teaching English. Henry was a chiropodist who ran a clinic three days a week with home visits for two. They had brought up their family and their grandchildren were either at Uni or settled into their careers. So now they had time for the first time to do as they wished. They decided on a holiday abroad. But where? And when? Not in the school holidays as it costs so much more and was so crowded.

They went to the library and borrowed some books to research places. In the end, they were attracted to Malta. A shortish flight, no language problems as everyone spoke English. The island was very interesting with its archaeological sites, boat trips to islands nearby and yet still had its own identity, although still touristy. They decided to stay in the capital, Valletta. It had buses all over the small island, boat trips and they would not need to hire a car. A very interesting old city. They booked for two weeks at a quiet hotel and looked forward to their first adventure in years.

"Will be like a honeymoon again," said Rebecca.

"As long as I don't have to carry you over the threshold," replied Henry.

The day came. Both hardly slept for the excitement. A taxi took them to Gatwick. On arrival they waited for their plane to show on the board. Eventually it showed up as being cancelled as it was too foggy to take off. They waited, but were eventually told they would have to stay in a hotel overnight, but free, luckily.

"At least we'd have a decent meal," Henry said "And a good bed."

Next morning was sunny and clear, no problems. The plane left on time and reached Malta in just under 4 hours. A taxi took them to the hotel in a quiet street near the town walls where they were warmly welcomed.

"We're really going to have a lovely adventure."

"The first of many, now we have time for ourselves," Henry said.

Rebecca went to shower, then let out a sigh.

"My contact lens has fallen out and I can't find it."

Henry was rather short sighted but couldn't see it either.

They crawled around, searching, looking under the bed and all around the bathroom with no result.

"Never mind," he said. "I'm sure we can get you fixed up here. Lots of good shops."

So off they went to find an optician. After an eye test, the optician said he could get one through by express the next day. The cost was about half the cost in England. So, all was well.

They spent the day exploring the city, with Henry reading out anything his wife found difficult. Next day she was fitted up and they went on to explore the George Cross Island with its own foods and snacks. Rebekah felt she was abroad, but relaxed as no language barrier.

They visited many sites dating back thousands of years. Went across to Gozo, a quieter, greener small island with its own character. Buses ran regularly and they went everywhere. At the end of the holiday, they decided they would go abroad every year.

"Next stop Venice and Florence." Rebekah would take lessons in Italian to prepare herself. They had both caught the travel bug and would take spare lenses and specs next time.

THE CABIN IN THE WOODS
Lorna

There was a light up ahead. Was it a cabin or was it something else? As we watched with bated breath, the light dimmed and then went out.

"Should we go and see If we can get directions there?"

As I spoke, I stumbled over the rough ground and almost ran into a tree.

"Careful," growled John. "No use breaking a leg now."

"Oh, do stop squabbling you two. I'm cold and wet and I want my tea."

That was Martha, always the practical one. We inched slowly forward to where we thought the light had been and became aware of the darker than dark of a building. We all gasped as there was the light again.

"I reckon that's the kitchen."

"Really. How can you tell?"

"Come on you two, don't lag behind. We need to speak to whoever is in there."

"Wait for me?" gasped Martha, the oldest in the group.

But before we could take another step, the light faded and went out.

"I'll go. You wait here." Bossy John loved to be in charge and disappeared round the corner of the building.

"I can hear voices," I whispered after a couple of minutes while we waited.

"It's alright, you can come in now," came John's voice from the dark. "We found the fuse box!"

IMAGINATION
Keith

"I have been waiting for nearly two weeks to be inspired or to get an idea that I can work with. Now you arrive, man/ woman, I don't know. What have you to say for yourself?"

"Well, I've been waiting," says he/she, "for you to let your writing juices flow so I can come to life."

"But where have you been hiding, may I ask? And what have you to say for yourself?"

"I must be like a ventriloquist dummy." says he/she, "as I can only speak and move through your brain. You must let me use your imagination to express my wants and needs. Just stop being 'in control'. Let your imagination float freely. What you write might at first be strange, but let my words come. You have been waiting for me to turn up, but I have been here all the time, blocked by your brain saying, 'Oh, you can't say that' or 'that doesn't make sense' and in time I just give up trying to breakthrough your defences."

"What can I say? It appears I have been blocking my imagination. If I learn to just let words come, I can discover a new freedom with words."

He/she says, "Yes, there is a whole community in your imagination. Let words flow as you did just now. It could lead to creative prayer. Your God is also in there. Ask questions. Write down what comes as answers. You might be surprised. Live free!

CHAPTER TEN
OUR SHORT STORIES

A REAL BOY'S TOY
Vicki

As it was a lovely sunny and warm afternoon, my boyfriend - no, I shall rephrase 'manfriend', (I haven't got to partner at this stage,) thought it would be nice to go for a stroll along the sea front. The sea was calm and there were a few children with mums and dads either swimming or paddling. Everyone looked like they were really enjoying themselves.

Our stroll took us along the harbour and we decided we would have a coffee and gaze at all the yachts and owners mucking about, cleaning or having small drinks gatherings.

We had just finished our drinks when we saw a crowd of people pushing each other to have a better view of what was going on, so we had to have a look to see what the excitement was about.

Eventually, we managed to get to the front of

the crowd, only to see a couple of salesmen demonstrating gadgets on a boat, and how they worked, of course. Lawrence was all eager to have a go, along with a dozen other men. This boat was 12 feet long and half the width of the length. It was sleek and very speedy. According to the salesman, it could do 45 knots from zero, which meant nothing to me. Miles, I understand, but 'knots' completely lost me.

Apart from the usual radar, radio and safety jackets, there were remote control, TV, laptop, that when using the remote control, panels slid across the dashboard and to the right of the steering wheel. There was a weather clock, a drinks cabinet at the back of a seating area which sat six people. Under the seats you could pick up the computer and mobile phone. The mobile alone had so much data you could contact the man in the moon.

I kept calling it a boat, but Lawrence said "It's not a boat, it's a yacht."

"It don't look like a yacht to me. That's what I call a yacht." And I pointed to this massive looking 'monster' which seemed to have a house on board. Laurence just shrugged his shoulders and went back to going over all the gadgets that were being shown.

I'm not sure how long he was enthralled with the instruments and spare parts, but it was long enough for me to mention I had a bellyful. Of course, Lawrence was so involved with other men chatting about it, about how fantastic it would be to own one of these themselves, that he was tempted to buy one.

Naturally, I had to ask him, "Where are you going to birth it? In the bath? A bit of a tight squeeze and will your pensions stretched to the upkeep and charges it will entail?"

Lawrence did seem so disappointed. I thought he was going to cry.

However, I did feel sorry for him. A burst balloon and a dream shattered. He was reluctant to come away from such a wonderful fantasy.

I've changed my mind about 'manfriend', boyfriend suited him better, the way he carried on.

It was sleek and very speedy. A real boy's toy. It certainly was that.

BEFORE REDMAN KING HOUSE
Dee

Before I came to live in Redman King House, I rented a flat in a big old house at the top of the long steep hill that leads to the Meads area of Eastbourne. The road ended in a T-junction, turning right took me to Beachy Head and left into the pretty village.

I was delighted to find this large flat with its enormous lounge with high ceiling and wide bay window. In the alcoves beside the ornate fireplace were two long windows so the room was always flooded with light. The icing on the cake for me of course, was the garden. It meant I could step outside my door for meals and coffees on sunny days. In one corner was a raised decking area that was a suntrap for relaxing. There was even what one can only describe as an overly large, glorified shed. I had great intentions of using it as a meditation room, but I never did get round to that, so it became a storage place for gardening tools.

While living in the flat, I continued my new career as a music therapist. I would take my keyboard into care homes and play the old songs for the residents. They would sing along with me, sometimes even getting up onto wobbly legs to dance. Some residents could be quite rude at times, asking when I would be finished or even one time throwing a shoe at me! I always kept my sense of humour and didn't take anything personally. It's surprising how music can influence the body and mind. My visits to the care homes would last about an hour and proved so popular that at one time I had about thirty homes on my books. It was rewarding and I enjoyed travelling to and fro in my little yellow car.

Sadly, two years down the line, the honeymoon period in the flat was over and the cracks began to show. I developed a cough and was quite chesty. Whenever I opened my wardrobe, I noticed a damp smell. On investigation, I discovered that the back of it was covered in green fur. The landlord sent someone to clean it and told me it was condensation. This wasn't something I agreed with. It seemed more than that to me.

When I had first moved in to the flat, a friend had advised me to put my name on the list for potential tenancy at Redman King House. A visit was planned and I did add my name though I was doubtful I would need a place there for many years yet. I was nowhere near needing hand rails and shower seats.

However, with the risk to my health in my present home, I now needed to look seriously at moving away. A letter was soon winging its way to Anchor, explaining my situation. Fairly quickly an answer arrived telling me that I would only be allowed to rise up in my position on the list if I became homeless. I wrote again pleading that my health was in danger and added that I was on benefits. The second reply came, repeating what the first had said. What was I to do?

Then about three weeks later, an envelope dropped through my letterbox. Redman King House had come up trumps and I was on the top of the list! This was such good news. The news got better in that, a few days earlier, I had looked at a third floor flat at Redman King House with a friend who had turned it down, reasoning that she was not quite ready to move. The flat I looked at with my friend was the one I was being offered. I jumped at the chance to have it, despite the hand rails and shower chair! I would ignore them.

The flat is on the third floor and in my opinion, it's in the best position in the building. When I open my curtains in the morning I am blessed with a wide-open sky where the swifts and swallows announce the beginning of summer as they swoop and dive to catch insects on the wing. The red brick buildings with their higgledy-piggledy roofs and chimneys climb up the hill to reach the tower block at the top. A landmark, though others would say it's an eyesore. At night the lights in the windows glow in the dark. I am very happy to be living in my flat on the third floor of Redman King House.

THE MAGIC OF TOADSTOOL DELL
Margaret

Arabella awoke in her bed of rose leaves and she stretched and yawned and looked around her. It was a lovely sunny morning normally, but this day had a dullness about it. She was off to visit Harebell Lane to see Cosmo, Mitzi and Will. They had agreed they would go on a search to find the secret of why the Dell was going dark and people were falling ill. They needed to bring the Dell back to the healthy place it once was.

Arabella leapt into the air, flapping her tiny wings like gossamer they were. She drank her early morning dandelion tea, then started on her way. She sent baby lamb on ahead with instructions to make sure they were up and ready for her arrival.

She arrived at Cosmo's Willow tree home and he gathered up his things that he would need for the journey, including the magic formula for the spell to help them call on the good witch Cymbel, Guardian of the Southwold. It was in case they were interrupted on the journey by the evil Andronia, the wicked fairy who, rumour had it, grew in size and strength every year.

Mitzi and Will lived next door to each other on Speckled Egg Way. They felt full of joy, love and happiness, good things to take with them as they went off on their journey to save the Dell from the evil forces that were making them all so ill and unhappy. They would need to be united, strong, and fearless.

The first challenge would be to travel through the Fields of Blades and Cobwebs. They knew Will had the cloak that made all things wondrous. They had a struggle at first, the fields were so dangerous for them and they were very afraid. Finally, they got through. The worst part was over.

They still had to go past the Waters of Despair. They had the boats of walnut shells. They were strong.

In no time at all, they'd crossed the water. Cosmo set up the things to make up the spell that would call Cymbel. Such a good, wonderful fairy to come to their aid. They were tired and so very afraid at times. They desperately needed her help. She could mix her Gallimaufry juice; they would then be healed. Then they would all need the second spell to rid the Dell of Andronia and her evil.

It was wonderful to see Cymbel at work. There was lightning, sparkles and huge magical clouds full of wonderful music coming from them. It ended with a spectacular screech and Andronia was no more.

Cymbel returned the four of them to the Dell, and blessed them mightily. Already the sun was fully shining again, shimmering on the leaves of the trees and flowers. The birds sang again. Happiness abounded once more. All was well in the Dell!

A HOLIDAY ROMANCE
Myrtle

It was another mid-summer silver evening, moonlight shining on swirling surf. Jack relaxed his shoulders, circling his head and loosening tense muscles. This Cornish holiday had begun badly - traffic jams all the way down from town, a list of broken equipment in their rented cottage, then the row with Suzie and her subsequent departure. That night, he had strolled the sands, picturing his troubles retreating with the ebbing waves. Watching the shadows disappear, he'd looked across at the rocks and seen the girl. She sat on the highest rock, her back towards him, her long pale hair tumbling over her shoulders and down past her waist. She didn't move, yet he'd been certain she knew he was there. At last, he looked away and when he turned again, she was gone, leaving the merest ripple in the sea beneath the rocks.

He'd come every night since, drawn by the mystery of her presence, her sudden disappearances. Tomorrow, he would be gone, back to his busy life, his perfect townhouse, without Suzie. Would he miss her there, undistracted by the fantasy of a girl who haunted his dreams? Once, she turned to look at him and he couldn't mistake the invitation of her smile.

His last night now, and she wasn't there! Impatient, he paced the shoreline, scanning the rocks in vain. She couldn't know, of course, that he'd planned to swim out to her. Feeling foolish, he turned to leave.

"Jack." Surf whispering on sand. How had she known his name? How had he missed her in the bars and cafes he'd searched by day? She swam in slow circles behind the nearest rocks, beckoning him. Abandoning shirt and shorts, he waded in, following as she headed out to sea. He admired her breath control as she dipped for long minutes beneath the waves, and then she was beside him. He felt the length of her, smooth and naked, except for her legs, which were wrapped in a slippery...what? Fabric.

She laughed up at him, then, pulling his face towards her and drawing him into a kiss. He snatched a breath as she pulled him down, down, and round him in whirling circles. His legs became entwined in long strands of seaweed, melding together like hers. Laughter bubbled from his lips as their bodies rose and fell, and fell again beneath the waves. Life as he knew it, was gone forever. Flicking his strong tail, Jack struck out into the open sea.

GRATITUDE
Dee

"I've got the job I wanted," shouted my husband. "We're going to move to Nottingham."

I flung my arms around his neck. It was such good news. We were living in a house that sat at the top of a very steep hill with a bus service that ran only once a week to the nearest town. With two teenagers, a toddler, and a baby I couldn't wait to find a house that was on flat ground with a decent bus service.

On my first day in our new house, I was excited to be able to walk straight down the road with my little boy to the local primary school. A shop and a bus stop across the road completed my idyll. It was the perfect life.

My five-year-old son made friends with some other little boys. Their mums included me in their chats and soon I was being asked along to a coffee and chat morning. It was the beginning of a wonderful friendship.

GRATITUDE
Lorna

Who hasn't had a hard time in their life? We all have. I think it's one of life's ways of getting us to grow up. For example: I went through a difficult relationship and many times vowed I would leave. But the prospect of what the change in my circumstances would mean kept me there. I told myself, if I stay a little longer, things are sure to get better, but they didn't.

Eventually, Life sent me a message via one of my outspoken friends. "You need to leave. Come and stay with me," she said, probably thinking she could teach me a thing or two. So, I did. I left.

Now, what could I possibly be thankful for? Looking back. On my attitude at the time, there was nothing I could be thankful for other than the pressure being lifted.

Other things followed. I got rid of so many of my worldly possessions because whatever I had, I had to carry with me on my back. That knapsack got so heavy I had to bow down to keep going. It tried to land me on my back several times before I had a bright idea get someone else to carry it for me. You know what? Suddenly I have no friends. It meant I had to think again, downsize again and again, and as soon as I had cleared a little patch, blow me down if I didn't find something to fill the gap.

My understanding of this story is that I wasn't supposed to stay in my cosy little home forever. Not growing, Not caring. Not feeling thankful, not living the life that was surely planned for me. And the more uncomfortable the relationships became, the more I thought, this is not my fault. It's there's, all the people that I didn't get on with. It's their fault. Until it was so bad that I left and found it pretty difficult to stand on my own two feet without the help and support of all those people who had helped me before.

But after a while I found I could walk all the way from South Africa to England via South African Airways, of course, and then, Life said. "Now it's your turn to uphold and support people." I became a live-in carer. This is not a job for everyone, and growing and adjusting to different people, all with their own life's challenges dragged me up by my shoe strings.

This is the crux of the matter. The question is, what can I thank each and every person who has influenced my life for, good or bad? What can I thank them for? What lessons did I learn?

LEAVING FOR LOVE
Dee

John Mason walked through the town he had lived in for all of his twenty years. He was a tall, proud young man who worked in the factory his father and uncle had formed in their youth. The pianos they built were renowned for their workmanship. But this day was not a happy one. His father was seething with rage at his only son. This was the person Mason Senior had been training up to take over the running of the business, and now he had badly let him down. John had fallen in love with a local singer who was now pregnant.

As John made his way out of the town, he turned to take a final look at what he was leaving behind. He would have to tell Mary that he had been disinherited. The onward journey would be a bumpy ride, but John was willing to lose it all for love.

THE THING I TREASURE MOST
Keith

I have thought long and hard about this composition. My mother never had a sewing machine, though always wanted one. I have already written about the view from my window. It's still green with a little bit of blue sky in the top left-hand corner.

So, what do I treasure most? I have questioned myself quite often.

What would I miss most if all my things were destroyed? I don't know. Sometimes it's this and sometimes that. So, I came to realise that the thing I treasure most is my thoughts.

Sometimes they are happy.

Sometimes neutral.

Sometimes sad.

So, are my emotions what I treasure most? No! Because by training my mind, I can change my emotions. By my mind, meditation and mindfulness can benefit me most. Therefore, I treasure my mind most!

WHAT I TREASURE MOST
Anna

It's very difficult to say which object I treasure more than another. My China cabinet contains all my treasured memories as well as a small perdoninum, (a small rosewood cabinet) that my maternal Grandfather made.

I have two very simply-shaped fish made by my granddaughter at primary school. Two bronze painted goblets that my dear grandmother had on a huge Victorian sideboard which was left to me but not released by my uncle for sixty years. A small chalet brought back from a Swiss school trip by my son, aged 9 or 10. a little plaque from my daughter that says, 'To Mother'. Lastly, a certificate won by my son for winning a hedging competition.

All of these I would grab if my apartment caught fire. All treasured and irreplaceable

THE THING I TREASURE MOST
Vicki

When I accepted Ken's proposal of marriage, after seven or more years of asking, he booked a table in an upmarket restaurant for dinner.

We chatted during the meal and laughed at things we had experienced during our life and marriages. We'd both been married before.

When the coffee was brought to us at the end of the meal, Ken gave me an object wrapped in blue foil and a blue ribbon with the most intricate bow. Blue is my favourite colour. It was wrapped so beautifully I was reluctant to open it. When I finally decided to, it was a book, 6" by 4", with a red velvet cover with letters written in gold - 'Love, a Celebration'. In between the pages was an engagement ring with a tiny blue bow threaded through the ring.

As I tried the ring on, Ken said, "Is it the right size?"

I said, "I don't need sunglasses for this diamond!"

He said, "You cheeky monkey. I meant the size."

When I accepted Ken's proposal of marriage, I did say I wanted an engagement ring. I never had one the first-time round, and it had to be a diamond that was so big I needed sunglasses to stop the glare. Ken took it in all good humour. The book, with its red velvet cover was a book of poems. I glanced at a few and they were so moving.

Ken said, "My favourite poem in the book is

'Always Marry an April girl.' It's the one at the beginning."

When I read it, I did have tears in my eyes. I was born in April. I got quite emotional. When I feel low, I get my red velvet book of poems and sit by the window and reminisce of years gone by.

'Always Marry an April Girl' by Ogden Nash

'Praise the spells and bless the charm.
I found April in my arms.
April Golden, April Cloudy,
Gracious, cruel, tender, rowdy.
April soft in flowered languor
April cold with sudden anger.
Ever. Changing. Ever true-
I love April. I love you. '
That's the thing I treasure most.

THE THING I TREASURE MOST
Dee

When I was about seven years old, in the 1950's, my parents enrolled me with the local dancing school. This was my dream come true as I had been pestering them from a very early age. Imagine my excitement when my teacher announced that we were to put on a show. We would be wearing incredible costumes. Heaven!

Mum was almost as excited as I was. There was nothing she liked better than to have a sewing project on the go. She wasted no time in offering to help make up the creations. Out came the sewing machine. It was soon almost lost amidst the yards of frothy netting and white satin fabric for the tutus. Ribbons, bindings, cotton threads, scissors, needles, and pins were added to the fray, often getting lost until Mum pleaded with me to find what she was looking for. Her trusty measuring tape was never far from her neck; her voice often muffled with a pin or two stuck between her lips.

One year bright green taffeta was used to create a knife-pleated skirt with a matching floppy bow for my hair. Tap shoes painted gold with green ribbon ties completed my outfit for 'The Yellow Rose of Texas.' Crepe paper was regularly brought into use, gathered, folded, and puckered into all manner of shapes: Easter bonnets, flower-petal hats, or frills on can-can skirts. Mum attacked it all with gusto.

Year after year the old sewing machine was brought out of its cupboard and put to work. As I got older, my interest in dressmaking grew. Material was relatively cheap in the early 1960's, making it easy for me to fill my wardrobe with my handiwork. My favourite lesson in school was needlework. I would choose a pattern, begin working at school then bring the item home to finish on our machine. I was so quick at my sewing while I chattered away, to such an extent that during one afternoon's lesson I was made to stand on a chair because I was distracting my much slower friends from doing their work.

I had to leave the sewing machine behind in 1965 when moving away from home with my new husband and eventually bought a new-fangled electric machine, leaving Mum with the old hand worked one.

In 1981, helping my parents pack up their belongings ready for their move to the USA, I unearthed the machine and asked if I could keep it. The black paint had lost some of its shine, but the gold scrolling pattern was visible. It even had a needle and thread, with the bobbin loaded. I couldn't resist placing a piece of material under the foot. Yes! It still worked.

I am so grateful to my Mum for the guidance and encouragement that I have passed on to my daughter. She is now the custodian of the family heirloom that is Mum's old sewing machine.

THE THINGS I TREASURE MOST
Margaret

The things I treasure most are family, friends, and freedom. The warmth, love and caring of family is impossible to replicate in any way.

The fun and laughter and stimulation of friends is irreplaceable. The meals out, the walks, the games also beyond compare.

All of these things filled with love represent freedom, because love is freedom. That intense inner warmth that builds good health, happiness, energy also a degree of self-care.

The giving and receiving, exchanging of love and laughter can only be achieved by the sharing of the many things we, as individuals think matter to us. These are the things that make our lives worth living, in my opinion!

CURIOSITY AND THE CAT
Vicki

Mitzy was a seven-year-old cat who thought she was three years old, the way she behaved with her mischievous ways. Mary had Mitzi from a kitten. Her granddaughter gave it to her from one of the litter her

Bonnie had. Mitzy was one of five. She got her name from Millicent.

Mary never wanted a cat but was smitten by the moggy with her front white paws and white nose, with the most beautiful Hazel eyes with a line on the bottom lids which looked like eyeliner. Over the years, Mitzy must have used ninety-nine and not nine of her lives.

Looking out of the window while washing up, Mary could see Mitzy at it again, stalking something she had seen on the table in the corner. It must have been a butterfly or a bee, not a bird as there was nothing on the table apart from two plants. Azaleas in their glory. Mary watched Mitzy slowly making her move and pounce on whatever it was and landed on the table, tipping it over and causing the plant pots to spread across the ground, then doing what she always did, run like a bolt of lightning to hide. Usually when it happens indoors, she heads for the back of the settee, like once she did when, being nosey, she jumped on the window ledge, smashing the vase of flowers onto the carpet, making everywhere wet. Or the time when she climbed onto the sideboard to investigate the painting of a fish in a tank. She climbed up like she does, bringing the painting crashing to the floor, after hitting an ornament on the sideboard which also broke to pieces.

How Mary put up with her mishaps, she couldn't say, but Mitzy was loving. She liked curling up on the settee with her head laying on Mary's lap, or purring away when she was stroked with her white paws padding up and down on her chest.

Mitzy was also funny, like the time she investigated a cardboard box which was laying around after taking some books out of it. Mitzy couldn't resist and got on her hind legs to see what was in the box, tipping the box over herself and going round in circles trying to get out.

What was nearly Mitzy's demise was the in the bedroom when she thought she would climb on the dressing table, knocking the mirror flying, which went straight across the floor, missing Mitzy by a fraction, just catching her back legs which made her meow and run like the blazes. She never stopped till she made it downstairs to hide in her safe place.

BEFORE AND AFTER.
Dee

She is smiling. Fiona realizes that it is the first time, except in photographs, that she has seen her happy. Before, there was always a 'before' and an 'after.' Before, whenever Fiona had visited grandma, she'd felt unwelcome. Yes, there would be the offer of a cup of tea, a piece of her delicious cake and an invitation to sit at the table. But grandma never sat with Fiona. She turned her back, busying herself at the sink or the cooker, clumsily banging pots and pans on the counter. She didn't make eye contact and would answer in monosyllables. Fiona often wondered why she ever went to see her grandmother.

As Fiona matured into an adult, she puzzled about Grandma's attitude and did her best to befriend the older woman, always hoping to tease out a snippet of what was in her background to make her so severe. The silence was frustrating. Even Fiona's mother was ignorant of her mother's childhood.

Grandma was a tall woman with a slight stoop, as though she'd like to be smaller. She held her head low over her skinny chest, rarely looking up. What had happened to her?

Fiona's curiosity was piqued when she was searching in her mother's home for some documents and came across an old photo album. Crouching down, she began to turn the pages. What she saw was astounding. Page after page of black and white photos featuring a laughing, beautiful young woman. Many photos showed her in a brief bikini, revealing her curvaceous body. In other photos she wore fashionable, flowing dresses, her long black hair falling like silk over her shoulder and there by her side, the most surprising thing of all was a tall, handsome man. They were obviously lovers as many photographs showed them in different locations, always looking into each other's eyes or laughing at the camera. The only reason Fiona knew the identity of the woman was that beneath each photograph was a caption revealing her grandmother's neatly written name. All other words had been scribbled over, blotting out any chance of identifying the mystery man. Something terrible must have occurred. Fiona had to find out.

Mum will know, she thought, but her mother didn't know who he was and claimed not to have seen the photo album. Fiona loved to fix things, to make right any wrong doing. Now she decided she'd find out why her grandmother was so sad these days, and who was her companion in those old photos. Maybe if she discovered the man's whereabouts, if he was still alive, she could reunite them. How fantastic that would be. What could possibly be wrong with bringing two people together after what had obviously been a very long time? The fact that his name had been scrubbed out didn't to deter Fiona from her quest one little bit.

A FINE ROMANCE
Margaret

As she strolled over the Downs, lost in her dreams, she saw a tall figure coming towards her. She couldn't believe her eyes. She immediately recognised who it was. She felt quite weak at the knees.

"Would he recognise her?" She thought.

How could that be possible?

To her amazement, as he approached her, he whispered, "My love, I can't believe it. It's you after all this time. It must be written in the stars. What a fine romance we have."

THE LETTER
Vicki

Molly hadn't been too happy these last couple of years, and Ted wondered if he may have upset his wife or done something he shouldn't have which put her in such moods. Nothing was right whatever he did, and the more he tried to fix it and make better Ted was put down. He loved Molly dearly. They had two handsome sons, a lovely home that Molly took care of. Oh Yes, she a wonderful cook.

Both sons did well, went to university, both passing with flying colours in their specified subjects. Sam was a biochemist and Marshall, a computer programmer.

Ted was sad because Molly was. He just was at

his wits end, not knowing what he could do to make life a bit more cheerful for her. He took her on holidays, surprised her with evening dinners in the best restaurants. Took her on day trips and the theatre. They went on a short cruise along the rivers and coast, including the Blue Danube, but nothing seemed to please her or to give her joy.

Then one morning, the postman delivered a letter, the usual postmark from America. She knew at once, of course, who the mail was from. She had so many over the last couple of years. When Molly opened the long envelope with her normal enthusiasm, she was already sitting down with her morning coffee.

When Ted arrived home for lunch, he had spent the morning in his club, playing snooker with some of his ex-workmates, he was surprised to hear Molly singing along with the radio, pottering in the kitchen, preparing a meal, looking much brighter.

Ted was speechless, so he said nothing but took his jacket off and made his way to the kitchen. Music was playing joyful songs.

Ted said, "Hello, sweetheart, You're in tune. I forgot what a beautiful voice you have."

Molly said in a bubbly tone, "Thank you, love," and pointed to the letter on the table where Ted always sat. Once seated, he put his glasses on and started to read.

"Molly, my darling, that is such good news. We must start to get things in order."

Molly is smiling, Ted realises it's the first time, excepting photographs, that he has seen Molly happy.

Marshall and Sam had written to say that they were both coming home to live for good. Two years was enough to be away from the family and friends.

BIRTH
Lorna

The ocean is troubled today. Steel-grey as the sky and broken like shattered glass. The icy East wind bit its way into my bones. My body shivered and shook of its own momentum. Uncontrollable. My heart and mind were numb with memories that flashed endlessly before my consciousness, reliving the poignant moments of pain, horror, abandonment. The crashing sound of metal upon steel. The screaming in pain that continued in the background, interspersed with other booming or high-pitched churning sounds near and far. Unexpected silence.

Then the continuing sirens like shattered glass again and again. The ocean that was so warm and friendly, comfortable, and safe is now gone and I give a cry of remorse, longing and outraged at all I knew and loved. All that loved me is now gone. In its place everything is icy, noisy, unloving, and painful. I am exhausted by the strangeness of it all. I just want to sleep. Fade away. Be gone.

"You have a son, Mrs Carmichael A healthy boy."

I hear these words behind my closed eyelids, but they mean nothing to me.

A MOTHER'S TALE
Dee

The little scallywag was up to his shenanigans again. He'd only gone and put salt in my tea. I'm flummoxed as to why he keeps getting into such mischief. He tries to bamboozle me into believing him innocent with his cute smile. He's a rapscallion, there's no doubt about it.

The other day he came home looking like a ragamuffin with his trousers torn at the knees. He's always getting into mischief. His teacher, oh Miss Whatsername, told me he causes such a hullabaloo in the classroom. He acts like a nincompoop, but he's actually a clever little whippersnapper. He's going to be in serious trouble if he keeps up this malarkey. When I asked him about it, he gave me a right tarradiddle. I couldn't understand what he was on about. If he's not careful, he'll miss out on the football thingamajig. Oh, what's it called? A try -out, I think. He's got all the gubbins for it, you know, the shorts, T-shirt, so he'd better start minding his P's and Q's.

THE LOST EARRING
Vicki

Leaving the theatre later than expected because of a taxi mix-up was a kerfuffle. The couple that was standing next to me and Pete thought it was their taxi 'til we explained we had ordered the taxi before-hand in the hope of the play finishing on time and giving ourselves an extra ten minutes to leave the theatre.

When we arrived home, we had forgotten that the hall would be in darkness as the bulb popped just as we were going out. Both my husband and me were stumbling about in the dark, bumping into each other. We made it up to bed and that's when I realised, I had lost my earring while getting undressed. I was quite annoyed as the earrings were a 25th anniversary present that Pete bought, knowing I love them when I first saw them in the window in the jeweller's shop in the High Street.

I fell asleep after a time of pondering where I lost the earring. Could it have been in the theatre, outside waiting for the taxi or in the taxi?

In the morning, I mentioned it again to Pete, but he was uninterested.

He said, "stop fretting, it's gone. I'll buy you another pair."

"It won't be the same having another pair."

I went in the bathroom to shower.

Pete called up the stairs, "Coffee's ready when you are. I'll start doing the breakfast. Don't be long."

"OK, darling."

Getting dressed, I thought, "what a lovely morning it is. Beautiful sunshine and blue sky. I'll ask Pete if he fancies a walk in the park later. We could have lunch in the cafe. They do really good meals."

Coming out of the bedroom, I stood at the top, looking down the staircase. Something glittering by the front door caught my eye, unusual for the sun in that area. Going down the stairs, not taking my eyes off the gleaming corner, I approached the lit-up section and bent down. To my surprise, there was my treasured earing.

NEW BEGINNINGS
Dee

My most momentous new beginnings have occurred following a roughly twenty-year cycle in my life. My wedding day, shortly before my twentieth birthday found me plucked from being a shy, naïve girl who'd never been away from home to becoming a married woman with a husband and home to care for, living many miles from my parents.

Twenty years later, on reaching forty I came to realise that the angry, punishing God I had feared for many years was actually a loving, forgiving Father. This realisation caused a monumental change in my attitude towards life and death. I regained my faith and became a committed Christian.

Reaching the maturity of sixty years, with forty difficult years of marriage behind me, I finally made a decision that was to be another immense new beginning for me. That decision was to walk away from the marriage. This new beginning was to give me the freedom to become the person I was meant to be. The real me.

Of course, within those momentous new beginnings have been other important new beginnings: the births of four children, the marriages of two of my children followed by the arrivals of five grandchildren.

From my birth in 1945 in North Wales, I have moved home fourteen times, changed schools five times, and changed jobs more times than I can remember. All lesser new beginnings but nonetheless significant changes for me to have to deal with.

Thinking of the twenty-year cycle, the next one is eighty years. I wonder what life has in store for me then. Only another three years to go!

I would like to encourage you all as loved members of my family, whatever age you may be, to tuck away the memories of your new beginnings and bring them out occasionally. Look at them perhaps in a new light, reflect on those moments and treasure your new beginnings as your greatest lessons in life. They are what made you who you are today.

BEGINNINGS AND ENDINGS
Keith

The sun is rising in Uganda. Light streams across Africa as the rim of the Earth slowly turns towards it.

What is moving" Me? The Earth? The sun?

This universe is a mystery. My African adventure is a mystery. Long before maps and compasses, people were more dependent on watching the sun and stars to find their way. They say that Africa was the womb of civilisation, that the first humans on Earth started here in Africa and wandered the world to find new homes and countries. They followed the sun and the night suns - the stars that seemed to inspire them. The wandering stars. They felt the stars were telling them things of life. Like the three wise men of the Christmas Bible story read in those stars - a King was born.

We have advanced now with all sorts of navigation instruments to find our way and tell of distant events, but you know, the stars shine on. The stars shine on.

THE STORM
Lorna

Andrew was born in the Eastern Cape, near East London. But, as sometimes happens in life, spent his formative years in the Transvaal. His grandparents had left England together with several members of the

McPhail family from Hambleton, near Alnwick in Northumberland. Their farm, Springfield, was huge by English standards. The ground was prepared and fruit trees planted, as well as fields of watermelon and other soft fruit. Andrew and his sisters, Mavis and Clare were given their own gardens and the job of providing the vegetables for the family and their attendants.

It was an idyllic lifestyle until the day of the storm. There was something about the clouds that gave the warning. The local people came running to the homestead.

"Mam! Mam! We must bring the animals in."

Soon everyone was running about, seeking shelter, making sure all the windows were closed and the children inside.

The Thunder rolled in, sounding like giants stomping about in the clouds. Then the wind came, dry and loaded with dust, and then big hard raindrops pouring down from the heavens, followed by hailstones advancing like a wall, closer and closer. Then overhead and onward. The sound was deafening, frightening, and strangely eerie. Green light filled the sky. Only then did the lightning strike, followed by a crack of electric thunder directly overhead.

The girls screamed and came running to Ma to be held close until the storm abated. Da and Andrew stood in the doorway, sheltered by the corrugated iron roof of the veranda, watching hailstones the size of golf balls bouncing, slicing, smashing, and turning the crops to mush.

As the storm moved away at last, a deathly silence was broken only by the seep and gurgle of the flooded ground and the whimper of little Clare in Ma's arms.

And so it was that everything had to be auctioned, and Ma stood under the Thorntree, watching with tears running down her face as her treasures were sold away for a few pence. Da packed the truck with tools, steel ropes and other hardware that was needed for the gold mines in the Transvaal and became a transport rider. Andrew, a gangly teenager, went with him. The journey was 1000 kilometres, (or 620 miles.)

As soon as Da had found a little house at Juniper Cottages near Johannesburg. The whole family moved to the Transvaal and a very different lifestyle.

THE WOMAN IN THE BLUE HEADSCARF
Vicki

When we moved into a semi-detached house, we being mum and dad and my brother, as teenagers not much of the surroundings was noticed. Although we had moved into a three-bedroom, neither Chris nor I was interested in what went on around us, as long as we were going out, having a good time with new friends.

Mum spoke of the next-door neighbour spending so much time in the garden and always wearing a pale blue headscarf, she noticed after two months of us living there that she never wore any other colour, only a blue headscarf. At the usual age of puberty, we of course weren't bothered in things like that. So, we let mum mumble on about our neighbour while we went out to have fun.

It wasn't till about five months later and so many made-up stories of the woman next door that my mum got the full life story. After wondering why, the woman always wore a blue headscarf and sometimes when sitting on a two-seater bench in her garden with a shawl round her shoulders a slight darker shade of blue was more curious to nosy mum.

She was a very quiet and shy woman, but pleasant enough to pass the time of day if she was to see us. Mum told us, when we were sitting at the table having a meal all about Alice next door. Apparently, Mum was in the garden hanging the washing and saw the neighbour sitting on the bench. The neighbour got up and made her way to her back door and went inside. Mum again wondered about her when the woman in the blue headscarf, as now that's what we called her, came over to Mum with a photo album and asked if she would like to have a cup of tea and a biscuit with her. Of course, Mother couldn't refuse as she wanted to know more about her and be a good neighbour.

Sitting in the kitchen, drinking tea, and eating biscuits, the woman in the blue head scarf started telling mum about herself. Eager Mum listened with both ears, with the odd Ooh's and Ah's. Her name was Alice.

My brother interrupted with, "It's Alice now, is it? I shall still call her the blue head scarf lady."

"Don't be cheeky," Mum said and carried on telling us that she had been married fifty-five years and two months when she lost her husband to a heart attack. Blue was his favourite colour and the blue scarf was the last thing he bought her as he said to keep her hair tidy when she's gardening.

Mum was thinking about the shawl she wrapped around her shoulders, hugging it tightly with both hands. Alice carried on to say how much she missed him even after four years and said to mother that she must think she's a silly woman because the shawl was a comfort to her, like having Tom's arms round her, like when they sat on the bench in the garden, listening to the birds chirping, he would put his arm round her shoulders.

Alice talked about her sons. Both lived in Canada, so she never saw much of them as she didn't visit anymore. Too much at her age of eighty-five.

Dad, me, and Chris were quite bored by it all, but Mum was in her glory not having to wonder anymore and surmise all things that were not true.

In unison the three of us in high tone voices said, "Are you now finished? Can we leave the table?"

"Pack it in the lot of you. I see you two want a clout round the earhole."

Dad raised his eyebrows with a smirk on his face.

Alice became good friends with the family, but Chris, being Chris, still called Alice the woman in the blue headscarf and always got mums tongue for being a daft 'apeth.

ARTIFICIAL INTELLIGENCE
Lorna

The long shadows of the morning drifted across the double lanes which once roared with the noise of heavy vehicles. The mist still clung to the planted windbreaks in patches, with streams of sunlight marking the sun's journey. It was going to be a hot day when all was clear and deliciously clean.

Now the sounds were of birdsong, a dog barking in the distance, and the quiet swish the all-electric vehicles sped elegantly along. No accidents for these remote-controlled cars. Some were occupied by a single person, but more were family size taking passengers to work or school. The odd ones were larger. Delivery vans of all sorts and the old public transport buses and coaches.

The speed was controlled remotely. One could almost say like clockwork, but that was long gone and only raised an eyebrow by youngsters who had not known about timepieces from a bygone age. Their voice-activated information badges built into the uniform, one-size-fits-all, gave them answers to any question they could think of. The only "fashion" was their colour choice. The material was self-cleansing, self-mending only in the remote off-chance of an accident such as being bitten by a mosquito or stung by a wasp.

Artificial Intelligence, AI as everyone referred to it now, was in use extensively. Children brought up in this way were taught good manners, discipline, exercise, and if they showed an interest in knowledge and hobbies, all this was at their fingertips. With the press of a button, voice activation would give the answers; play music, or provide live simulated activities such as tennis or football. How to play the bagpipes, or sing opera, dance Swan Lake, or make old fashioned cookies. All these were there for the asking.

As I stood gazing pensively at this new world, The Electronic Revolution, some were calling it, I thought back to the olden days, when a visit of 100 miles say, to spend Christmas with my grandmother and all the family, would take four or five hours, depending on which of my parents was driving. The roads were often bumpy and there was always a chance that we could have a puncture or the radiator might run dry, but that's a thought for another day. Below me on the motorway, the gentle throb of passing traffic was most soporific. I blinked and found I had sat down and dozed off, leaning against the barrier. The sun was up. It was time to go home.

NE'ER CAST A SHOE
Dee

When I was very young, I loved to dance, especially tap. My mother bought me a pair of tap shoes. They had a metal plate screwed to the underside that made a wonderful noise when I flicked or stamped my feet. When she bought them, they were black with black laces. So boring. Hidden amongst the pots of paste and packets of sequins in her storage cupboard was a tin of gold paint. Before I could blink, she had transformed my tap shoes into magic dancing shoes.

I wanted to dash off to my dancing lesson as soon as I put them on to show off my wonderful new shoes. As I reached the door, my mother grabbed my hand.

"Ne'er cast a shoe, 'til the sky is blue," she scolded. I stopped in my tracks and looked up into her eyes with anger. How could she spoil my excitement?

"What do you mean, mother?" I pleaded. "I want to dance in my new shoes. What's the colour of the sky got to do with it?" My mother pulled me into her arms and kissed my head. It's an old saying. It means that you shouldn't rush into things before you are ready.

I still didn't really understand what the words meant, but I trusted Mum. I knew that I had to practise my tap steps to be ready to show off my new shoes when the time was right.

THE RESCUE
Keith

One of the most difficult rescues I feel must be from deep caves, I am reminded of the rescue of the boys and masters of the football (or was it cricket?) team from a cave. The country escapes me, but it was led by a British cave rescue leader and international team.

The boys and teachers were trapped by a sudden flooding of the cave and it was thought they might not have survived.

The rescuers had to work through passages so tight and water so deep, they had to find and sedate the boys to get them through the deep water to go ahead, to escape from what could have been there tomb. But they made it a great adventure with only one fatality of a rescuer

THE VOLCANO
Anna

The ocean is troubled today. Steel grey as the sky and broken like shattered glass. Toby was planning to go fishing. He sold fish daily to the Islanders who relied on him to supply good, nourishing food for their main meals. They had plenty of fruit and vegetables and a few pigs and scrawny fowls, but fish was their main staple. Toby looked up to the volcanic crest some miles away, some tiny wisps of smoke drifted up to the cloudy darkening sky, yet still the sun shone mutedly. Toby decided that it would be alright to go out now as long as he kept near the shore. Plenty of fish, prawns, clams there as well as smaller fish. He let down his nets and lifted them. Nothing there. No seething mass as usual. The volcanic smoke had increased and the sea began to look threatening.

Quickly he turned back and with a little help, anchored his boat high up the beach. He hurried to the head man of the village.

"I think we are in for a dangerous time. The volcano is beginning to wake up."

So, the head man called to his steward to sound the alarm. A series of large gongs which were struck in time to call the villages to meet up. As a small island, it could be heard a good distance and distant Islanders would be passed the message. When everybody, all 100, had gathered, Isaac, the village elder announced that the volcano was looking threatening. It had happened about every 50 years, so the people knew what to do. Isaac told them to gather up the few animals, children, people, and provisions and go to the caves high up the small mountain. There was no danger yet.

The men went to make safe their canoes, the women to gather the children and goats, chickens, dogs, etc. They knew exactly what to do, so off they went in a procession, each giving assistance where needed. Almost like going on a village picnic, arriving safely but wearily at the chain of deep caves. They were used to times of trouble.

Water dripped through a far corner and shelves cut in the rock face were stored with basic foods, rice, lentils tins of soup, dried apricots and other fruit and matches well wrapped. Also, tin mugs, plates, kettles, and a large saucepan. Enough to survive on for a short while.

There was a long labyrinth of caves. One could easily get lost there. Small divisions, so each family could have a little privacy.

How the children loved exploring, running around, and squealing in delight. The grown-ups set about making a little home in the cells as best they could. The animals were penned in a large area away from the humans. So, they all sat down to wait in safety. Slowly, gradually, after a few days, the volcanic smoke died down until only a small, harmless puff of smoke remained like an old man's wispy beard.

The village elder decided that all was safe and they could go home. Everyone cleaned up and packed up and in a long procession returned to the village. Rather sadly returning to their daily chores after their little respite, but glad to return safely. Stores in the caves would be renewed to be ready for the next invasion, a real haven in times of danger.

THE AFGHAN BLANKET
Lorna

I sat quietly in the passage of my neighbour's house. I could hear her talking, but not what she said. I wouldn't have understood it anyway, as I knew she was from Afghanistan, as my daughter had told me.

I was in a sombre mood, my thoughts filled with my own troubles. Loneliness, guilt, a sense of loss that brought tears to my eyes, unbidden and uncontrolled.

"My dear lady, what's the matter?"

My thoughts were shattered by the entrance of the Afghan woman who put her arm around my shoulders.

"I'm sorry, I'm sorry," I said, wiping away the tears.

"Come and sit in the lounge and tell me all about it."

She held out her hand to help me up and we went into the next room. It was a beautifully decorated place and the crocheted blanket over the couch caught my eye immediately. The colours were so cleverly matched or in contrast. The little details of the flowers and inter-spaced squares which joined the larger tiles were fascinating in their myriad combinations. I couldn't take my eyes off it. I felt like a sponge, absorbing every detail. And slowly my sadness left me and I knew that there was hope. Hope for better things to come. Hope for healing for my loneliness, and hope that one day, not too soon, but not too far in the future, like this blanket, my life could once again reflect the different colours of my experiences, good and bad, happy, and sad, glorious, and shining with memories.

A cup of tea appeared before me. I looked up into the smiling face of my new friend.

"I know you have had some deep sadness and I wish you every happiness and healing," she said.

"Thank you, my dear. I feel the presence of my beloved husband, all the animals I have ever loved, and my heart is comforted by you and your blanket. I am not alone anymore."

THE AFGHAN BLANKET
Keith

I got out of Afghanistan just before the Taliban took control. I didn't have time to pack. I just grabbed what I could and fled. It was not until I was in a safe place, that I opened my large travel bag to see what I had saved. I must have grabbed the most colourful thing I could see. That beautiful Afghan blanket filled most of my case.

When I spread the blanket, I was taken back to the time I watched my mother creating that wonderful blanket. I experienced again, feeling my mother wrapping me in that blanket for the first time so long ago, just like yesterday. Her very life is in that blanket before the Taliban took her life because she protested at their new laws against women. I wrap myself in love and her blanket.

THE AFGHAN BLANKET
Anna

It belonged to my grandmother, who escaped from the village when the Taliban destroyed it. The only item she managed to save. It is now with her in her children's home in India, where she now lives in safety after fleeing from Afghanistan. The blanket was made by her mother, so very precious to her. I remember her sitting by the fire in the evenings, wool picked up cheaply in the market. All the colours of the rainbow and the countryside around us. Patterns are copied from the Persian rugs. When finished, I loved it on my bed, so soft and cosy.

When my mother died, it was as if she was still with me. Then came the war and no one felt safe.

Eventually all from the village had to flee and hide and try to get away. My son and his family paid money to have me secretly brought to them in India,

I was safe and hoped to start a new life in peace. Their way of life was very different. Different foods, culture, but their neighbours were so kind to me, giving me the things I needed, like clothes and bedding.

At last, I could relax without fear, my blanket wrapped around me and it was as though my mother was there comforting me, protecting me, making me smile, and restoring happiness. I need no other thing now. It will be passed onto my only granddaughter and I shall tell her all about my life as I grew up with the blanket. A lovely heirloom!

A CHILDHOOD MEMORY
Lorna

Sharon Gawronski, a fat Jewish girl who sat behind me in class. We had double desks, wide enough to hold two children. I had my best friend Avril Edwards next to me. The teacher was out of the room and the class had become loud and unruly. Sharon started poking me on the head with her ruler. I didn't like it, but kept quiet, watched by Avril, who was clearly annoyed and concerned for me. But Sharon kept it up, getting harder and faster, trying to provoke a reaction from me.

To this day, I don't know why I let her do it, and it was Avril who couldn't stand it anymore and told her to stop.

Now, all these years later, I realised what a debt of thanks I owed to my friend. At the time, I was too numbed to do or say anything. I can't even imagine what prompted Sharon to start her torture. I didn't know how to deal with her aggression. Her skills at anger management were lacking development. Or perhaps she was treated in the same way. It has been a puzzle whenever I think of this incident, to fathom the motive, the part Avril played. And what about me? What did it say about the way I dealt with this unexpected aggression?

A WALK IN THE COUNTRYSIDE
Anna

The long shadows of morning drifted across the lane, lighting up the valley and bringing a glitter to the river. Birds began their morning worship of praise for another day. The windows on the old cottage began to smile with the coming sunlight. The countryside began to stir, greeting the new day. I could hear sheep in the distance bleating and saw the small herd of Jerseys being guided to their field for the day. A dog barked and wriggled joyously as its master came into the farmyard.

"Where are we going? What to do?" the dog seemed to indicate. As I walked along, following the narrow track across fields and over the headland, I breathed in the cool, fresh air. Life was good. I had a good pack of food, water, stout boots, and the promise of a lovely sunny day ahead. England at its finest. I would not wish to be anywhere else, not even on the long treks through foreign parts, however startlingly beautiful. Give me the quietness and peace of England.

I could see a few small boats on the sea, maybe local fishermen out on the still, calm water. A nice fresh, fish supper for me tonight.

After a few hours I found a very convenient set

of rocks to sit on and to take a break. How much better, food tastes in the fresh air. A simple roll with cheese and onions. A sweet crunchy apple to follow and wine-like water to quench my thirst. The sun warmed my back. But if I sit too long, I shall not make it down to the hostel for the evening meal. Somewhat reluctantly, I continued my walk. Being September, then nights had begun to draw in. I passed a small wood with rabbits and squirrels darting around. Fun to watch their activities. Then the track began to go down to the village about two miles away, making walking easier. Down I went and felt compelled to enter the small thatched, very old pub I came to. A pint of local beer was like nectar. Worth all the long walk. My reward. Then onto the welcoming hostel, full of other walkers all eagerly chatting about their day.

I was fortunate to obtain a room of my own. Small, cosy, very neat, just basic needs, but all I could want. A hot shower put new life into me. Then to join the others at the communal table for a wonderful local fish and chip supper and tea by the gallon.

The end to a very special, perfect day. What more could a man want? Just a good night's sleep, to waken to a new day and new adventure.

Goodnight all, sleep well.

WHAT DO I DO NOW?
Keith

It was early evening, a week after her first appointment. She said she was feeling rather tired after our evening meal and wanted to go to bed. This tiredness had been growing over the last two months. I'd advised her to cut down her work at the factory and to see the doctor about taking a safe stimulant.

Her doctor had advised a course of treatment over the next six months. She wouldn't tell me what it was.

She went to bed. I said I would clear things up downstairs and have an early night myself.

It was getting on for 9pm when I ascended the stairs and found her there on the floor of our bedroom. She had pulled the pillows and eiderdown with her, cushioning her fall and, I think, for comfort.

I tried to rouse her but there was no pulse. I was lost. I hadn't learned what to do for her. I just phoned 999 for the ambulance. The police came and questioned me about what happened. They took her away after they had confirmed she was dead. Now I'm waiting for the post-mortem.

What on earth happened?
Who's responsible?
What do I do now?

THE RED FLAG
Vicki

Sitting on the beach on a lovely hot day. Sunny and blue skies. Watching all the swimmers and paddlers enjoying the cool water made me want to join them, but I had no towel or swimwear and didn't want to paddle. I had nothing to wipe my feet on.

It was such a gorgeous day. The beach was packed. Some having ice cream. And there were others with their hats or brollies protecting them from the sun. Some were having sandwiches and flasks of beverage. There were a few other bathers drinking pop or alcohol, making the best of the weather. There were plenty of surfers and speedboats, even a lonely yacht made an appearance. The children made the best of making sandcastles and even someone was buried up to their neck with sand.

Loads of laughter and screaming went on, but what a fun time. It was so full of activity that when the red flag was showing parts of the closed area, every surfer sighed with disappointment. But it never stopped them having a good time.

FLORENCE
Anna

Florence makes the heart beat faster. It is such a lovely city. Everywhere you go there are spectacular sights, like the huge statue of David. Huge, cave-like churches with enormous oil paintings, lovely gardens around them, birds, and butterflies.

Alas, everywhere is too crowded and noisy, not allowing one to view anything in peace. If one wanders off down little cobbled streets, one can see the real city, how ordinary people live.

I found the river Arno, much-mentioned in the last war. Everywhere is an atmosphere of friendliness and welcoming, Italians are not afraid to show emotions.

After a very hot and exhausting day, back to the hotel for a glass of wine, dinner, and a rest before plunging into the city the next day. One could spend a lifetime here and still not see everything. There is so much life here, such passion and joyfulness, it really enters your heart, especially out of season when one expects it to be quieter and hopefully more peaceful. I would so like to return. Dear Florence.

MISHAPS TOO OFTEN
Vicki

I called round to Maz, my friend of many years to see if she was ready to go to town. She already had her coat on when I arrived, locking up and putting her keys in her bag. We were off to the opticians. We didn't take the car as it was a pleasant walk through the park and not too long to the shops.

Reaching the opticians in good time we got the lift to the first floor. Neither of us had been to the shop before, so when the lift stopped, we stood there waiting for the doors to open.

I said to Maz, "I think the doors are stuck. Just then we heard a voice behind us. This way ladies," and turning round there was a young man standing at the lift doors.

He said, "Come to the desk, I will book you in for your next test."

We said, "Thank you," and sat down giggling. What daft fools we must have looked.

After leaving the opticians we decided it was a good time for lunch, so we strolled over to our favourite eating place, managed to get a table in the corner by a window. After making up our minds what we would have to eat, Maz said, "Would you go to the bar and order our drinks while I clear the table."

Sitting down bringing a bottle of wine with me, I told Maz our order will be about twenty minutes. Chatting and giggling about the lift incident, I pulled the wine and passed the glass to Maz. On doing so, my arm caught the bottle and I knocked it over. It went everywhere. Down my trousers and part of my top. Glad it was me and not my friend.

After lunch we made our way home through the park, both of us looking up at an old tree, pointing to the bird's nest that looked like it was ready to fall. We never saw the small branch lying across the path. We nearly tripped over.

"Things do come in threes so we should be alright now," Maz said. "We don't want mishaps too often."

"Too right," I said.

Once we got to the front door, Maz couldn't find her keys. She looked everywhere. I knew she had put them in her bag, I saw her do it. After a good ten minutes turning everything out of her bag, we still couldn't find them, until Maz remembered taking them out of her bag and putting them in her pocket when she was looking for her glasses in the opticians.

Once in the house, we thought we both needed a strong cup of tea after the events of the day.

My friend said, "Comes in threes? In our case, it came in fours."

TALL TREES
Keith

I think I have told you of this before, so I'm very sorry to bore you again with my favourite garden, Wakehurst Place in Surrey. It is in East Grinstead, and I visited it quite often when I lived and worked in the Quaker retreat, Claridge House in Lingfield, Surrey. The reason I write about it is because I'm looking forward to going there next week for a retreat. What reminded me and forced me to write about it was my first two words, 'Tall trees'. The tallest trees I have been with - American Redwoods, 300 ft high or taller.

On one visit to Wakehurst, I was feeling broken-hearted from the break-up of a relationship. It started raining and I sheltered under what I now call 'my tree'. As I pressed my back against the soft bark, my heartache just melted away. This happened a year later when my ex-wife wrote to me of the death of our two cats. My bereavement went deep. I went straight to 'my tree' in Wakehurst and the same healing balm happened again. So next week I will be with 'my tree' again.

THE CABIN
Anna

There was a light up ahead. Was it a cabin or something else? I had started off on a long walk following the cliff path. It was much further than I guessed and getting darker with every step. There was no path down to any village where I could find a bed for the night. Suddenly, through the trees, I could see a glimmer. At least it must be some sort of habitation. Even if only a barn. I hurried up and found it was a wooden cabin with a welcoming light above the door. I knocked and the door creaked open. In I went.

A wood stove was burning. On it was a gently steaming kettle. The table held plates and bowls covered over. And the simple bed was made-up against one wall. Very warm and cosy, but uninhabited. Very strange. As though ready for a visitor. I warmed myself by the fire, took my boots off and settled down to wait.

I felt sleepy but didn't give in as I was waiting for the owner to return.

Suddenly I heard dogs barking and then heavy steps up and into the cabin. A very tall thin man came in. He had an awful scarred face and yet look cheerful.

"Hello," he said. "I was hoping someone would drop in suppers ready."

He made a big pot of tea, uncovered the food, thick crusty bread and put a pan of soup on the fire to heat.

"I'll just feed the dogs and put them in the stable," he said as he left.

On his return, we sat around the table eating the lovely soup, bread, and apple pie. With a cup of tea, we relaxed and chatted.

"I get few walkers here," he said. "But like to be ready in case someone drops by. My name is David. I was in a prison camp in Singapore and only managed to survive with cunning and luck. They treated me very cruelly, so now I like to live on my own with my two dogs in peace and quiet. I write for a living and make enough for my simple needs. How about you? What do you do?"

I hesitated before speaking. My English was good, but I knew if I talked, he would be upset. I am Japanese, but I'm also a pacifist, hating the way the atom bomb did so much damage to my people for generations.

He looked very strangely at me, making me feel fearful and uncomfortable. What would his reaction be? What would he do? The cabin was in the most solitary spot. He had control over me. Yet the man appeared relaxed and had a gentle manner.

He began to tell me his story. He had trained as

a doctor and obtained a job in London before an opportunity opened in Singapore just before the war. He had worked in a clinic in the poorer area of that beautiful city. Although many rich lived there. there is always an underbelly of poor and disabled who can't afford doctoring. He had met leprosy, typhoid, and all manner of tropical diseases. How he had enjoyed the life and had met many more remarkable and clever people. So many had clung to the old folk medicines and treatments which were often dangerous.

So much he learned, an exciting journey. Doctors are much respected and however poor; he was given some precious tokens of their thanks. A piece of delicately embroidered cloth. An apple or orange or banana.

David, as he revealed, was there for four years and met a sweet nurse from the area. They married and ran a small clinic. Then disaster. The Japanese overran Singapore. Many fled, but more had nowhere to go, so had to stay to face the absolute hell. David and his wife were imprisoned in different camps. He never saw her again. He was put in the labour gang. Backbreaking work, beatings, scarce food and only 'slops'. Men treated without care, only as living nuisances with great disdain. For a nation loving children, how could they be so cruel?

David, being a doctor, was unable to help anyone which wounded him more than others. There were one or two guards a little more compassionate, who at great danger to themselves would secretly pass him a bandage, or Quinine or. painkillers, so he could ease a little of the problems. Men grew weaker, fell, and died. Fights broke out over a crumb of mouldy bread or a rotten banana. It really was fight or die.

A couple of times David was put in the 'hole', a dugout cell with no shelter, just the scorching sun for a day or two. No food, no water.

Still, he struggled on for three years. Then one morning when he woke, no stamping feet, no shouting. No guards. Was it the end of the world? Everyone crept out, expecting to be shot down. Nothing. Eeriness. Then friendly lorries drove in. Freedom. The war was over. News from outside. Cheers from the sick, poor broken souls. They could wash, drink, and even eat a little. Have treatment for all their illnesses. For many it came too late, but at least they would die in peace and a dignified manner.

David said to his new friend, "I think I have gone on long enough. It's 11 o'clock. Let's sleep on it and I will tell you more tomorrow."

He made me a comfortable bed on the floor by the fire. In my sleeping bag, I slept until daylight crept through the window.

David roused and went outside to wash at the pump, even in the chilled water. Dressed, he came in roused the fire and put on the kettle. I was so cosy, calm, and refreshed. I wanted to stay safe in my nest, but felt obliged to get up and go out to wash and dress. The dew was still moistening the grass, but the sun was warming up the backyard. By now coffee was brewing and bread being toasted. What a deliciously simple repast. We said little, slipping quietly into the day. I helped David tidy up and put his home into order.

The dogs had been fed and let out, and were now patiently waiting their master to take them for a walk. We went off over the hill to a village about 3 miles away, where a small shop supplied the simple needs of the local folk. Lovely crusty bread and cheese purchased and milk. The owner had a supply of dog biscuits ready for any canine friends visiting which our dogs appreciated.

Off we went across the area of downland with panoramic views of the sea. Sounds of gulls squabbling, joyful birdsong and buzzing bees created a fine symphony around us. The air was like pure wine and the grass was speckled with sweet smelling wild flowers. Could anything match the countryside in Spring? We walked on in comfortable companionship. Words seldom needed. We returned to the cabin to enjoy coffee, bread, and cheese. A heavenly feast!

We then relaxed outside Me to doze and David to get down to writing his book. In the evening, I felt I must really get down to telling and admitting my own background. Not an easy task. I actually slept for two hours Until the sun moved round and a cool breeze sprang up. So inside to supper of bacon and eggs and a thick slice of crusty bread, followed by a piece of apple pie. Bliss!

As we sat around relaxing, David asked me about my life. What did I do? Where did I live? Not prying, but in a very gentle, caring manner, I said I was called Yuki. I confessed that I was also a doctor and specialised in paediatrics. I was Japanese and have a practise in a small town about four miles from Nagasaki. I had had a wonderful wife, my soulmate, and a four-year-old daughter. We lived well and were respected as a family. I loved my work and was able to help improve the lives of many children.

Then came the war. I was sent to a hospital for servicemen. Such different work, but I came to enjoy it. I was very sad that after patching up the men, they were put back into hellish battle again. So many had been recruited and hated war. Poor simple farmers torn away from their homes. Peace loving men who had no choice but to give their lives for the emperor. I too hated the futility of war. So many deaths, so little gain, so much despair and helpless left behind. So, I did what I could with very limited resources. I listened, comforted, and helped write letters. Of course, some men were arrogant and deemed it good to serve the emperor, hoping for recognition and reward, dead or alive, but mainly men were considered only as common cannon fodder. Expendable.

I fought the new morals in silence to prevent any reprisals towards my dear family. Eventually the war drew to an end with so many repercussions, suicides and increasing hardships. The Japanese pride and empiricism being trodden down. The Americans blasted Hiroshima out of existence. The horrific effects lasting generations. Did the USA really know what horrors, the bomb would cause? I doubt it. If that wasn't enough, another bomb was dropped on Nagasaki. It was quite a bit later, I heard that a huge area was affected by fall-out as well as the destruction.

My living nightmare was the danger my family were in. No news, no contact, my own living hell. When at last Japan surrendered, I was able to leave the hospital and make my way back to our village. I could not get more than several miles near it for over a year because of the dangers. I was nearly going crazy with worry and fear. At last, through the Red Cross I managed to learn that no-one in my home area had survived. There was definite evidence of that. I only wished my loved ones had died suddenly and without pain.

Life was black and hollow. What was the

meaning of it all? What had been gained? I almost lost my mind, too horrific to imagine. I had a breakdown and was in a blissful coma for awhile. The doctors in hospital got me through and I began to live again. Gradually I took up the reins of my profession.

I came to England, to a Children's Hospital and began to heal. I vowed I would do what I could to make up for some of the cruelties inflicted by the senseless wars. So now I am on a pilgrimage to find deep inner peace. And to move on.

You, my friend, seemed to have regained piece. I would like to stay awhile, if I may. Just to rest in your company. Maybe I can pay penance in some way for your loss. We must have long talks together. Now I'm tired and have revealed a lot about myself. The night draws in, and I'd just like to sit and relax before I retire.

We sat in companionable silence until the clock struck ten, then prepared for a peaceful night's sleep. I actually slept until the sun woke me at seven. The best sleep ever. David already had the fire going and the coffee simmering. Bliss1 For breakfast, he cooked slices of local bacon and a duck egg each with fried bread, a gourmet's feast, washed down with wonderful coffee. After cleaning up, David hung out our bed clothes on the hedge to freshen up. A lovely, warm spring day.

I looked around the garden area. David had spinach and a few cabbages ready but other vegetables to come later and a few fruit trees. He had a pretty little flower bed with Snowdrops, Daffodils and Elephant Ears in flower. A Rose climbed up one wall of the cabin and over the front porch grew Honeysuckle. Real home-like. The view over the undulating hills was uninterrupted, but only by trees and a very distant farm, such peace and quiet. It flowed over one's soul.

I went in and gave David a hand tidying and cleaning.

"What can I do to help?"

He replied, "Well, I have to keep in a good supply of wood for the stove. Today, I'm going to find some branches to bring back to saw. With two of us, we can get a goodly amount."

We walked about a mile or so to the forest, plenty of fallen branches and kindling here. Together we carried the wood back to saw and to store. A stop for coffee, then to work. David had a fine sawing horse he had made, so that made it easier. But sawing is hard work for me, not used to manual labour, so I was given the job of splitting the logs and stacking them in his barn.

We sat outside in the sun and enjoyed a fine meal of bread, cheese, and pickled onions with an apple. The dogs running free, came back and were given a few biscuits, then ran off again. They seem to appreciate their freedom and safety here too.

After our snack we finished the wood job, made ourselves comfortable and had a little siesta, sheltered and warm in the sun. I feel so at peace, like warm water gently washing over me. The stillness and lack of demands, relaxing my inner core. The past horrors and sorrows gradually dissolving day by day.

I easily slipped into the daily routine of hard manual work and restful periods. Time slipped by as if on oiled wheels. I realised I'd been here for three months. Sometime I must return to the harshness of the world. I will need to earn money for everyday living. I would have to continue with my vocation as a paediatrician, but to work with those with the greatest needs, maybe in the Third World. So, I spoke to David as we sat by the fire, well-fed and relaxed.

He wisely said, "I feel you are now much stronger and am able to return to the outside. Go out and follow your heart. There is a plan for all of us, but we must not be in a rush to just jump into the first opportunity. Wait and you will find the answer."

So, I packed my few belongings and left two days later, sadly but full of hope for the future with my soul and body healed. I walked to the nearest local bus and took a ticket to a new life. I found a small hotel in the nearby town where I could begin to find the way to my answer. Reading the newspaper, I felt that where I could be of real help with children, was in Africa. HIV was rampant, so many orphans, so many tropical illnesses and other life-threatening diseases. Yes, that was my calling. I had to refresh my knowledge on these matters. So, after six months, I applied for a vacancy in Kenya in a country area. Patients could be brought there by local buses, ambulances or even on the back of motorbikes. Rural, but not impossibly isolated. The hospital had good supplies, about sixty beds and was well staffed and well run by the devoted matron, all of whom could speak some English. I was given a two-roomed brick bungalow so could have some space for myself. Perfect. I would learn Bantu or whatever as I went along.

From day one I was welcomed and made to feel at home. Parents could visit the children or stay overnight if they lived far away, sleeping on mattresses on the floor. They could help with some basic nursing and learn how to care for their children when at home. The orphans lived in a separate building and were well cared-for and educated. What I loved especially were all the children's sense of fun, happy smiles, and gleaming white teeth. It was difficult to settle in, learn the language and ways of treatment in a very different environment and climate and culture. However, I was helped so kindly by another doctor and the nurses. The heat was something to become used to as well. Living areas were very basic. Just a thatched rondel. Water was rationed and lavatories were basic to say the least, a box with a seat over a big hole. One soon adapted and everything was kept very clean by the house staff. Food was basic too, depending on what vegetables were available with occasional meat but wholesome. A much simplified but adequate life. One saw many cases of children with malaria, pneumonia, usual children's illnesses, but inoculation was happening which lessened the infections. There were also problems like hare-lips, which were much helped with operations, burns from fires, TB, HIV which responded well to Antibiotics usually. Much depended on the weather during the dry or wet season. We had a few cows and chickens to fill out our rations. Life was basic but not uncomfortable. I stayed at this hospital for two years until I was affected by severe malaria. I became so ill that it was necessary to send me back to England when I was somewhat recovered. Sadly, I left the hospital and returned to England.

I have been in contact with David all this time. We are very good friends now, almost like brothers. He invited me to stay and recuperate in his cabin. So, there I was again enjoying the peace and stillness of the woods and countryside. What was I going to do? I needed money to live, however simply. I didn't know. I was not in a fit state to decide now. I just had to get my body fit again.

This gradually happened and an idea began to

form. Somehow, I would provide a retreat and safe place for servicemen suffering from post-traumatic stress. Maybe have my own cabin built for this.

Eventually this occurred. I bought a piece of land in Cornwall and had a Swedish-type cabin built with four bedrooms, a large garden and near the coast. We could grow our own produce, have chickens, and maybe have a pony and cart to meander down the quiet lanes or to the small village, a mile or two away.

My first recoverees are due soon. Two mentally and physically handicapped young men, sent back from Afghanistan. Life has changed, but offers a rewarding future to all of us. We can all share the peace and natural healing and the men will be able to talk out their fears and be released from their day and nightmares in a caring atmosphere. In helping to heal them, I shall be healed too. In peace we can live and share and be able to move on as whole souls again.

THE AFGHAN BLANKET
Dee

A market town, England, 2020
Grace puffed impatiently as she danced from foot to foot.

'Mum, this is taking so long. There's nothing to do or see. All the shops are closed and I'm hot and thirsty.'

This was their allotted time to leave their home for essential items. For the past five weeks, Grace and her mother Eileen, had walked from home to join the long line of customers shuffling forward, keeping two metres apart and wearing the obligatory face masks and gloves. The world was in the midst of a Corona Virus pandemic. They were queueing on a street lined with shuttered shop fronts, barred doorways and litter strewn around. One shop stood out among the others; a charity shop, or as Grace liked to call it – a curiosity shop. She had to be patient, hoping they would be able to stop outside her favourite place. At last, there it was. Her eyes scanned the objects openly displayed. So many exciting and mysterious things. It was a feast after being locked in the house all week. Twinkling bracelets and brooches; a baby doll with such a sad face that Grace longed to go inside and rescue her. But the best object of all was draped across an old armchair. It was a rainbow-coloured blanket. Eileen told her it was an Afghan blanket.

Grace pressed her nose against the glass. She turned her head from side to side as she noticed one of the patches had sparkling yellow threads that glittered like gold. The sun, brilliant in a cloudless blue sky, caused the colours to glow. Reds, purples, yellows, blues, and greens of different shades. Sadly, the door was shuttered and bolted with no sign of when it would be open for business again.

She was so eager to discover answers to the questions whirling around in her head that as soon as they reached home, she went to her computer to investigate all she could find about this word, Afghan. It intrigued her. She was amazed to discover that it came from the word, Afghanistan and was a country. The people who lived in that country were called Afghans. She learnt how they suffered terrible things because of war; that many thousands had died and were thrown out of their homes. Grace was shocked to discover that families were forced to flee over mountains in all weathers, crossing the border to refugee camps in

Pakistan. The young girl thought she should never complain again about having to wait to buy their food and stay home because of the pandemic.

Grace lived with Eileen in a small house on the edge of the town. She'd been attending the local primary school until the Corona Virus pandemic hit the world. Now she and her mother stayed home. Eileen had always worked from home and recently had set up a table butted against her desk for Grace to work at her lessons. They enjoyed each other's company and with the help of the internet, Grace was soon happy in her new routine of working with her mother.

After she'd rushed home to find out about the Afghan blanket, she couldn't stop thinking about the children living in that faraway country. What must it feel like to have to run away from home and live in a different land? If that happened to her, what would she grab to take with her? She had read that many people had died. Children were left without parents. How would she live without her mum? Totally alone. She couldn't bear it. She vowed that when she grew up, she would find ways to help those refugees. Then she had an idea.

'Mum, what if we made an Afghan blanket and sent it to the refugee camp? Could we do that? Can you teach me to crochet?'

'Slow down, darling! It's a lovely thought but it would be like giving a crumb to a starving man.'

'But, Mum. You always say to me that it's the little things that make a difference. Surely this one little thing could help one family. Maybe keep them warm at night. Does it get cold at night in Pakistan?'

'When we looked at the map, we found the Peshawar refugee camp was near the mountainous area of Pakistan, quite close to the border with Afghanistan, so I'm sure it will get very cold at night.'

'So, shall we? Make one? If I get good at it maybe we could make more.'

'Hey now, don't get carried away. And what's with the "we"? I'll teach you how to crochet but you've learned so many things on the internet, there's bound to be someone with a video tutorial for a blanket. You never know there might even be one for an Afghan blanket. That could be your next lockdown project.'

The next day as she sat at her desk opposite her mother and looked around the room, she smiled. It really was a happy room. She could see pretty flowers through the large patio doors and when they were open on a sunny day, bird song brightened her heart. Although she missed her friends at school, she couldn't help but be glad she was able to be in this room. Every morning, she would log-on to her school's activities planned for that day, she could see and speak to her friends too and her teacher was there with answers to her many questions. She decided to tell them about the Afghan blanket in the shop window and about the things she had learnt.

Eileen ordered packs of coloured yarn and crochet hooks from the internet and had soon shown her how to work a chain and some basic stitches. It wasn't long before Grace found a tutorial for an Afghan blanket that she could follow. It was with determination that she persisted, choosing colours at random from her stash of yarn. She needed to make twenty 'tiles,' finishing off with the small triangles and diamonds to join the whole lot together. Her idea blossomed and caught the imagination of her teacher who suggested to the rest of the class that if any of them felt able, they could join in the project.

Now, whenever Grace saw the blanket in the shop window during a visit to the supermarket, she inspected it closely, imagining how her own blanket would look when it was finished. She was so pleased to think she might be helping a family all those miles away with a life so different from her own privileged one.

She was making great progress, when one morning she stopped in mid-stitch and dropped the crochet hook. The look of dismay on her face, alarmed her mother.

'Darling, what's the matter?'

'How will I get the blanket to the refugee camp in Pakistan?'

'Oh no, we hadn't thought of that. Grace, I'm so sorry'

Her mother paused, tapping the end of her pencil on the desk.

'In the days before this pandemic it would have been easy with lorry-loads going to and from the camps. But now, nothing is being allowed to move.'

'Yes, I suppose so,' came the mournful reply.

'The main thing is you are making it and we'll have to hope that the lockdown will ease soon and then we can find out how to get it to Pakistan.'

'Well, I'm determined to finish it and perhaps I'll just go on making more until a better time comes. And with my friends joining in we might have a lorry-load one day.'

'Good girl. If you can keep up that positive attitude, you'll go a long way.'

Peshawar Refugee Camp, Pakistan 2020
Afsoon woke with stiff aching limbs and a bigger ache in her stomach. Her three younger sisters and brother lay

on the dirty brown blanket beside her, snuffling in their sleep. As usual, she was the first to waken. She threw her hijab over her head and across her face as she set about her first task of the day. A fire needed to be lit so that she could cook the daily ration of rice. The water pump was a five-minute walk along the dusty stretch of land that led between the rough shelters that her countrymen called home. She was glad to be wearing the hijab as it kept the dust from her hair and made breathing less difficult. Warily, she watched a stray dog that lay in the early morning sun, yawning to show yellow teeth. To Afsoon's left, was the camps rubbish tip where items that had become useless were dumped. The camp children searched every day for anything that might help their families. Things like an old rusty pot for cooking or something that could be used to stir food in the pot. They became adept in being creative with the things they found. To them, nothing was useless.

As Afsoon approached the water pump, something colourful caught her eye in the tip. On investigation, she found it was an old knitted sweater. It had several holes in it, but was so bright it made her happy. She smiled to herself as she picked it up and placed it round her shoulders before making her way to collect the water. Carefully, so as not to spill a drop, she rushed back home. By now, the children were awake and her father was sitting on the ground outside the doorway. This morning, Afsoon didn't notice how bedraggled and old he appeared, or how his eyes didn't acknowledge that she was there. No, his daughter was excited to show her sisters and brother the sweater. They shouted at once that they wanted one too, but Afsoon shushed them as she had other ideas about it. They would never find enough sweaters for each of them and anyway, anything they found would be full of holes. 'What shall we do with it then, big sister?' Afsoon kept quiet as she dropped the rice in the water. Instructing her next sister, Gulnoor to watch it, she dashed off again, this time to a different area. She knew exactly

what she wanted. It took some time before she found it. Afsoon hoped that Gulnoor had been a good girl and not let the rice boil dry. It was too precious to have it stick like glue to the bottom of the pan. Reaching home, she inspected the rice and saw that it was just right.

'Well done, Gulnoor.'

After they'd eaten their meagre share of the food, Afsoon settled the children to play with little stones she had found and went to sit beside her father. Back home in Afghanistan, her father had been well-known for his wood carvings. She knew he still carried one remaining precious knife, so taking the stick out of her pocket, she held it in front of him. As if coming out of a trance, he turned his head to look into her eyes. He was spell-bound by the light in her beautiful eyes. But more than that, his heart pounded as he reached out to touch her face behind the veil. He almost thought he was seeing the ghost of his beloved wife. There were the green eyes of Afsoon's mother; the ferocity and determination that had her fighting for the lives of her children as she was held at gun-point back in their village in Afghanistan. She won that fight but lost her own. Tears began to slide down Taimur's cheeks. Now, here in this dreadful place they were forced to call home, their twelve-year-old daughter had fallen into the role of madar to her siblings.

The girl was impatient with her father's

sentimentality.

'Father, will you make me a crochet hook out of this stick?' Afsoon pleaded.

When her mother had been alive, she'd taught Afsoon to make blankets with crochet hooks. The sweater she'd found had given her the idea to make a blanket, just like the ones they'd made in Afghanistan; blankets that they'd had to leave behind in their haste to escape the bullets. A blanket would be for all of them, a sweater couldn't be shared. She would make a game for her sisters to collect any bright yarn from the tip. She'd ask her father to make more of the crochet hooks and if he agreed, she'd teach her younger sisters to help make the shapes that would create the blanket. It would be a myriad of colours and textures. Once it was made it would keep them warm and snug during the cold nights.

Now she sat at his feet, waiting for his reply. He gazed into the distance with unseeing eyes, deep in thought. Taimur was a quiet man, wanting only to feed his family and protect them from danger. In his opinion, he'd failed. Before the pandemic, he'd walked each day with his handsome young son, Shahmeer to the market the refugees had set up, working to help traders in any way he could. His reward was a few coins, rice and leftover scraps of fruit and vegetables. Now, because of the pandemic, the work had dried up. The market-place had been abandoned and they had to rely on hand-outs from the Pakistani government; something that no Afghan man felt comfortable with but there was no choice if they didn't want their families to starve. He was brought out of his reverie by Afsoon tugging on his sleeve.

'Will you do it, Father?'

'Where is this stick? Did you find a strong stick?'

Afsoon held up the stick again for her father's inspection, holding her breath. Without the hook, she wouldn't be able to put her plan into action.

'Yes, daughter. You've found a fine stick.'

While Taimur whittled the stick with Shahmeer sitting close by, watching his father's every move, Afsoon gathered her sisters together and told them about her game. Before long, they'd returned with handfuls of bright knitted bits and pieces.

'Where did these come from? Who threw them away?' Shabana, her youngest sister asked.

'Before people became ill, rich people from all over the world sent us parcels of clothes. They came from places like England and America. I think the people who threw them on the camp tip have died or maybe their child has grown too big and can't wear them anymore. But we're going to make the most beautiful blanket you've ever seen. It'll keep us warm at night. Would you like to help?'

They all agreed, nodding their heads with wide earnest black eyes gazing in awe at their amazing big sister.

Peshawar Refugee Camp November 2033
Grace dropped her rucksack on the dusty road as she jumped down from the lorry. She stretched her arms above her head, arching her back to ease the ache she felt all over her body after sitting in the lorry for hour after hour of bumpy travelling. But she was ecstatic at having finally arrived at her destination. Inside the back of the lorry was a mountain of packing crates, crammed with blankets of every shade and hue.

Back in England during the pandemic of 2020, Grace had set in motion a drive to crochet Afghan blankets. She'd been resolved from the age of twelve to strive to gain knowledge of the conditions and lives of those living in the refugee camps. Through school and university, she'd continued with dogged determination to reach her goal to make a difference to the lives of dispossessed human beings in the world. In 2033, she'd achieved a position of UN Ambassador. Now here she was in one of the biggest and oldest refugee camps in the world.

Afsoon, looked up from her cooking pot, baby slung in a shawl across her hip, when she heard the rumble of engines. The sound still bothered her, but she knew this was not a threatening engine. Along with her neighbours, she made her way to where the incoming lorries would stop to drop off their loads. The women chattered excitedly together, laughing, and clutching onto various children. She spotted the white woman standing beside the lorry, her blonde hair blowing off her face in the breeze. Afsoon thought she was the most astonishing person she had ever seen. A man was there too and Afsoon assumed he was an interpreter. She longed to speak with the woman from that mysterious world beyond her imagination.

The crates were being unloaded and carried into a large building that had been built especially for storing goods that were brought in from outside the camp. Everyone was curious as to what had been brought this time. Afsoon pushed her way forward until she stood in front of the blonde woman.

Addressing the man, she said with a nod toward Grace, 'Please tell her my name is Afsoon and ask her who she is?'

After listening to the translation, Grace replied, 'My name is Grace and I have brought you blankets from England. Would you like to take a look at one? I have one in the cabin.'

Before Afsoon could take in what the woman had said through the interpreter, Grace was standing in front of her again. Shocked at the agility of this person, Afsoon was even more shocked when she saw what was in her hands. It was a blanket bearing the same pattern that Afsoon had been making out of the threads of yarn she and her sisters collected from the camp tip. A pattern that had been passed down through generations of women.

She grabbed Grace's hand, turning to push through the gathering crowd. Reaching her home, she stooped through the low doorway and immediately emerged, holding her own blanket.

They laughed until tears rolled down their faces with a mutual understanding, closing the gap of hundreds of miles between their two worlds.

Printed in Great Britain
by Amazon